Gymnast Gilly
The Novice

By the same author

Gymnast Gilly – The Dancer

PETER AYKROYD

Gymnast Gilly
The Novice

Illustrated by Annette Olney

**DRAGON
GRAFTON BOOKS**
A Division of the Collins Publishing Group

LONDON GLASGOW
TORONTO SYDNEY AUCKLAND

Dragon
Grafton Books
A Division of the Collins Publishing Group
8 Grafton Street, London W1X 3LA

Published by Dragon Books 1986

First published by Grafton Books
in hardback 1986

ISBN 0-583-30777-9

Printed and bound in Great Britain by
Collins, Glasgow

Set in Times

Chapter 1

There it was, slapped on the wall above the door in
ugly great letters of red paint for all the world to
see:-

GYMNASTS GET OUT

'It's horrible,' said Gilly Denham to Marcia Cherry. 'It makes me feel sick. What loony would want to do that?'

Marcia agreed. 'It's crazy. What has the gym club done to deserve it?' She added as if to console any other club member who was listening: 'At least whoever it was got their spelling right.'

Gilly ignored her, her mind reeling in disgust. Someone did not want the Lincston Gymnastics Club to move into their new headquarters and this was the most obvious way of telling everyone in the club – gymnasts, coaches, parents.

The two 12-year-olds were standing in the car park at the end of the building which was new for the club but old in age. It was a disused factory which had been built at the beginning of the century in red brick on its narrow site between Manton Street and the canal. Its structure seemed small and low, but it was long enough to hold two tennis courts with plenty of room to spare.

Most of the other old industrial buildings in the area were being pulled down to make way for new factories and offices. This building had been saved, because without too much expense it could be converted to take on a new role as a base for the thriving Lincston Gym Club. That was the club's plan, a necessary plan if the club was to grow. But now the red paint gave notice that that plan did not suit everyone.

What loony indeed? Gilly shivered. She never dreamed when she became a gymnast two months

6

ago that the club with all its friendly people could have any kind of enemy . . .

Gilly was fair-haired, dark-eyed, with a big mouth that smiled easily. Her favourite sport was gymnastics. Ever since she was a toddler, she had loved to jump, somersault and cartwheel from sheer joy. The furniture in her home in the Midlands suffered a great deal as she was always bouncing or crashing on beds and chairs.

Her parents had endless patience. They knew that as she grew older, her energy would be spent on other activities.

Her father once remarked to friends: 'We soon learned to move all our ornaments to higher shelves.' However, the ornaments stayed there until Gilly's younger brother Richard was well passed childhood because he tried to copy her.

When Gilly was six, she happened to see a big gymnastics tournament take place on television. She watched spellbound as the gymnasts, in brightly coloured leotards, vaulted, somersaulted and danced in a series of daring yet graceful movements. She knew there and then that she wanted to become a gymnast – a top gymnast who could perform just like the girls she had seen.

Her parents discovered that the only way Gilly could become a successful gymnast was to join a gymnastics club. Unfortunately, there was no club at Hammond Primary School where she was a pupil and there were no established clubs within easy reach of the Denham home.

Naturally, Gilly was very disappointed at this, but

in the meantime she decided to find out all she could about the sport. She began a scrapbook in which she pasted newspaper clippings of the exploits of international stars at the Olympic Games and World Championships. She watched leading gymnasts compete on TV whenever she could. And she read library books about past and present world greats such as Olga Korbut of Russia and Nadia Comaneci of Romania. She also read gymnastics magazines so that she knew many facts to do with the sport in Britain as well as in other countries.

Gilly continued to practise her cartwheels and handstands but she still had not joined a gymnastics club by the time she was twelve.

'Be patient, Gilly,' said her mother, 'you're still young enough to learn how to become a good gymnast.'

Gilly sighed. 'That's just it, Mum, I'm not. I should have started serious training when I was eight. Most expert gymnasts do, and some even begin before that.'

Then her whole world changed. Her father was transferred by the engineering company he worked for to Lincston just outside London and so the Denham family eventually found themselves in a new, sunny home near the centre of the little town.

At the same time, Gilly had finished her primary school education and as a result became a pupil at Lincston High School. The High, as the school was called, had been founded over a century ago and was situated in a large grey building which looked like an old hospital.

At first, Gilly felt the High was like a prison. It took her a few weeks to get used to the size of the school with its hundreds of girls and for some time she felt very lonely, particularly as she did not have any friends in Lincston.

She looked forward very much to the PE classes in the hope that she could take up gymnastics but Lincston had a strong tradition in team games such as netball and once again there was no school gymnastics club.

However, she noticed that one girl of her year had, like herself, a natural ability for sport. What was more, the girl seemed to be an expert in gymnastics as she could perform back flips and round-offs.

'A round-off,' Gilly told Richard, 'is like the cartwheel except you bring your legs together when you are upside down and make a quarter turn to land facing the direction you came from.'

The girl at the High had the same brown eyes as Gilly but had almost black hair and the kind of skin which tans quickly under the sun. She was also very friendly.

One day, she noticed Gilly watching her open-mouthed after she had performed two back flips in a row across the school gymnasium, 'Hello,' she said. 'I'm Marcia Cherry. Please don't think that I am showing off.'

'Of course not,' laughed Gilly. 'I just wish I could do back flips like you can. I'm Gilly Denham, by the way.'

'Well, I've only just learned to back flip – thanks to the gym club.'

'What gym club?' asked Gilly, her eyes open wide with interest.

'The Lincston gym club, of course.'

A whistle blew as the PE teacher strode in to organize netball practice.

'Look,' whispered Marcia, 'why don't you meet me after school for a milkshake or something and I'll tell you all about it.'

'Great!' said Gilly as a netball flew into her hands. 'See you later!'

After school, the two girls met in the Moo-Moo Milk Bar in the shopping centre on the way home and Gilly heard from her new friend exactly what the Lincston Gymnastics Club was.

Sucking noisily through a straw, she asked: 'How long as the club been going?'

'I'd say about two years. It's now got about 100 members between eight and 16 – all girls. We've also got 20 coaches who do the instructing and many parents who help to run the club by doing odd jobs like looking after the equipment or raising money.'

'All the members must be at different levels,' observed Gilly.

'That's right. Most of them do recreational gymnastics which means they do it just for fun and don't train so hard. But there are three squads for gymnasts who want to take the sport seriously.'

Gilly stirred her milkshake. 'How do those squads work?'

'Young beginners are in one squad, then there is

10

the novice squad for people like me with some experience, and finally the top gymnasts are in the elite squad. Everyone tries to get into the elite squad because they have advanced training and go into the best outside competitions. And I can tell you, the club is a very friendly place whatever squad you're in. What gymnastics have you done?'

Gilly explained that she had never belonged to a gym club and although she could do cartwheels and handstands she felt that she was now too old to begin proper training.

'Nonsense!' cried Marcia. 'I know of a couple of British champions who started at our age. You'll know of them, too – Avril Lennox and Suzanne Dando. And they both performed in the Olympics.'

'I'd love the chance of joining your club,' said Gilly wistfully.

'Well,' said Marcia firmly, 'come down to the club tonight and have a look. Then make up your mind definitely whether you want to join, because becoming a gymnast is not all that easy.'

As they walked to catch their buses home, Gilly learned that the Lincston Gym Club was based in a church hall but was just about to move to its own headquarters in a converted factory.

'You see,' Marcia told her, 'the hall is now much too small for the club. Worse still, all the equipment has to be taken out of store and assembled before each training session and then taken down and put away afterwards. You can imagine what a waste of time that is!'

So John Hanley, the chief coach, and the coaches

11

and parents on the club committee decided to find a larger building which the club could buy for its own and where the equipment could stay in position all the time. After a long search, the factory was found and bought with money collected from fund-raising activities and grants from the council and sports organizations.

There was still a lot of work to be carried out on the factory before the club could move and parents and members were using their spare time on jobs such as carpentry, painting and plumbing.

'Any jobs you're good at?' asked Marcia.

'I can sew a bit,' replied Gilly with a grimace, as sewing was not exactly one of her favourite pastimes.

'Good,' said Marcia, 'we'll have you working on the curtains. Anyway, I'm sure it won't take too long to finish the conversion work. Hey, there's my bus. My dad and I will pick you up about seven o'clock.'

When Gilly arrived home half an hour later, her mother could see her excitement.

'You look pleased as a monkey with a bag of nuts. What's up?'

Gilly explained that she was going to the Lincston gym club that evening with Marcia to have a look around.

'Tell you one thing,' said Mrs Denham, 'you're not going anywhere until you've done your home-work. Is this club the sort of place you've been looking for?'

'I hope so, Mum,' said Gilly as she took her school books upstairs to her bedroom.

A few minutes before seven, a car hooted in the road. Gilly looked out and saw Marcia waving. She ran downstairs, grabbed her anorak and kissed her mother goodbye.

'Enjoy yourself, darling,' said Mrs Denham who was watching television.

In the car Gilly met Marcia's father who, like his daughter, was wearing a striking yellow tracksuit. 'I help out with the coaching at the club every now and then,' he told her. 'I hear that you're a bit of a gymnast already.'

Gilly repeated what she had said to Marcia earlier on, saying that she would love to be what she called a real gymnast.

'You better talk to Christine Nesbitt,' said Mr Cherry, 'she's the coach in charge of the novice squad.'

When they arrived at the church hall, Gilly could see why the club had to move. That particular evening's training was just for the novice squad but even so there was very little space for the equipment and for performing the various exercises. All the 15 girls wore the club's yellow tracksuit with the badge of an animal's head.

'Is that a cat on the club's badge?' asked Gilly as she sat down to watch members and coaches bring out floor mats and a vaulting horse from behind the hall's stage.

Marcia snorted. 'Yes and no. It's a lynx, which is a sort of cat. Can you guess why it's on our badge?'

Gilly could. 'Because it's in Lincston – the name of the club.'

13

'Well done, Gilly. Now I must join in the warm-up. That's Christine Nesbitt, the coach in charge. You'll meet her later.'

A tall young woman with her hair in a pony-tail clapped her hands and led the novice squad in a series of exercises performed to music. Gilly knew that all gymnasts must warm up their muscles to make them relaxed and stretched before starting any training or competition. Hard exercise with 'cold' muscles could lead to injury.

The mass warm-up was the start of an evening of energetic activity which went on non-stop for two hours. After the warm-up, the girls took off their tracksuits to show that they were all wearing yellow leotards. The coaches then split the girls up into several groups which in turn practised different movements, some on the pieces of apparatus such as the vaulting horse, others on the floor mats.

Many of the exercises had to be repeated again and again, and Gilly could see that many people would consider that training for gymnastics was just too boring and tiring. She herself longed to join in, but she knew that she had to wait until she became a member.

After the session, Mr Cherry introduced her to Christine Nesbitt, the novice squad coach.

'So you want to be a gymnast, Gilly?'

'More than anything, Miss Nesbitt,' said Gilly.

'Do you realize that as well as learning the four pieces of apparatus – the vault, the asymmetric bars, the beam and the floor – you have to spend a long time preparing your body with exercises. Why?

Because a gymnast must be strong and supple, and have plenty of stamina. And it's only you who can decide whether you are going to succeed or not.'

Gilly looked the coach in the eyes. 'I know it's hard, hard work all the way, but I know that I'll get there once I have the chance.'

Miss Nesbitt smiled. 'Then we must get you on the waiting list. A lot of girls want to join the club and you'll have to have a test some time. But don't expect your test too soon.'

Gilly was delighted. She felt like leaping all over the hall. She knew that she was not in the club yet, but going on the waiting list meant that she now had a very good chance of becoming a member.

Marcia was happy for her, too. 'You could pass the test blindfolded. I found it very easy – and I didn't even know what the club wanted in its new members. I have a better idea now, and I can give you some hints at school.'

As the Cherrys drove her back home, Gilly resolved to try many of the exercises which she saw being performed that evening. She was going to be prepared for the test, whether it took place next day, next week, or whenever.

And even if she failed – heaven forbid – she knew that she had found someone who was going to be a good friend, whether as a gymnast or not.

Over the next few weeks, Gilly ran to the front door of her home every time the postman came. Her brother teased her about it.

'Hard luck, Gilly, the old gym club have forgotten about you. They won't test you in a million years.'

15

He had to dodge out of her way quickly to avoid a clout.

With Marcia's help, she polished up basic movements such as forward and backward rolls and practised the splits every day, trying to keep her legs in a straight line level on the floor. She had found performing the splits uncomfortable at first, until she became more experienced.

'All gymnasts have to perform the splits properly,' said Marcia in her role as coach. 'It can be used as a movement, leap or pose. That's not bad – you've got much better at it.'

Then one day, the postman became her best friend. He brought the long-awaited invitation which had been in her thoughts every day. It was brief:-

Lincston Gymnastics Club
Your test for admission to club membership will take place next Saturday at the Church Hall at 3.00 P.M.
Clothing: T-shirt and shorts
Please let me know if you cannot attend.
John Hanley, Chief Coach

Whoopee, thought Gilly as she turned a cartwheel for joy, Lincston Gymnastics Club, here I come! Who's going to stop me now!

Chapter 2

That morning at school, during their history class, Gilly told Marcia about her coming test at the gym club.

'Saturday?' whispered Marcia. 'That's great. You're bound to do the same movements that I did, and you'll find them dead easy – ' She broke off as Mrs Allan, the history teacher, glared at her.

'Marcia and Gilly, I would be grateful if you communicated with each other after this class and not during it.'

Blushing, the two girls returned to their books and immersed themselves once more in the industrial troubles of 19th century Britain.

During break, Marcia hurried up to Gilly. 'Look, how much work have you done on the beam?'

'None at all,' replied Gilly. 'Why?'

'Because walking along the beam is one of the movements you'll have to do.'

Both girls stood in silence, each knowing what the other was thinking. Gilly knew that she should practise on the beam, yet finding one to use at such short notice was almost impossible. Marcia realized that outside centres where gymnastics took place, very few gyms would keep this unusual piece of equipment which was 5m long and only 10cm wide. The fact that the beam is 1.2m above the floor makes it very daunting for the young gymnast, and Gilly was aware that the test at Lynx would show how inexperienced she was on this apparatus.

'We've got four days,' said Marcia slowly, 'we'll come up with something.' She turned to Gilly. 'In the meantime, practise walking along any narrow surface that's above the ground – walls, planks, that sort of thing. It will be better than nothing. But take care as you do it.'

18

Gilly remembered something. 'There's a wall along the school carpark. Would that do?'

'Of course it would. You get out there after school and just walk up and down it.'

So Gilly did. The wall was about the same height as a beam even though its top was twice the width. Even so, Gilly did not feel secure at first when she began to walk on it. She now knew that performing on the beam was not as easy as expert gymnasts made it look. She concentrated hard on keeping her balance as she moved along and as she turned about, ignoring the puzzled looks which members of the school staff gave her before they drove off in their cars.

'You're doing fine,' called Marcia across the carpark. 'Keep it up.'

Gilly gave her a nervous grin. 'I haven't fallen off – yet.'

'You won't if you keep your mind on it,' said Marcia. 'Hold your head up. Relax your arms.'

'You sound like a coach,' said Gilly as she wobbled on a turn.

Her friend smiled. 'Perhaps I'll become one later on. Steady there! By the way, I've found something that's going to help you a lot. I'll show you tomorrow.'

Gilly practised on the wall for another hour before she and Marcia went home. 'I think I'm a lot better already,' she confided as they waited for their buses.

'We'll see you a champion yet. Come to school a little early tomorrow and we'll carry on.'

19

The next day, Gilly met Marcia in the school gym before assembly.

'Look what I've found,' said Marcia with pride as she pointed to two old school benches by the end wall. 'Now you can really get the feel of the beam. I've got permission to use them, too.'

To Gilly, the benches were far wider than the top of the wall she had walked along the day before. 'How can they help?' she asked.

Marcia caught the disappointment in her voice. 'Don't worry – just help me turn them upside down.'

Gilly was amazed. There, on the bottom of the bench at floor level, was a narrow strip of wood which ran along the middle connecting the three supports.

'It's just like a beam!' cried Gilly happily. 'You are clever!'

'No, I'm not,' said Marcia. 'They have a couple of benches at the gym club which they use in this way for beam practice. Now let's turn the other one over and place them end to end. Then you can start work.'

For the next four days, Gilly came into the gym as often as she could to walk along the upturned benches. She knew that in no way could she expect to become confident on the beam in such a short time, but at least she now had some idea of the balancing skills she needed.

Marcia agreed. 'You'll certainly have no trouble passing on the beam tomorrow,' she said as they left school on Friday afternoon. 'Just keep your head – and look happy about it. That's very important, believe you me. By the way, I'm coming along to see how you do.'

On the Saturday morning, Gilly's mother sensed the feeling of panic which her daughter had about her test at the gym club. 'Come on, girl,' she said firmly, 'you're not going to perform in front of millions of people. If you hate the thought of performing in public, then you should give up the whole idea of becoming a gymnast.'

'Oh, Mum! I couldn't give up now!' Gilly felt better after that but she still had a fluttery feeling in her stomach.

At last the time came to go to the club. Gilly put on some navy blue shorts and a yellow T-shirt which she thought was close to the yellow of the Lynx leotards and tracksuits.

'Good luck, Sis,' said Richard while her mother gave her a hug. Gilly's father had arrived back from a business trip so he gave her a lift in the family car.

'Got your hymn book?' he asked when he saw the Church Hall. Gilly thumped him on the shoulder and told him about the club's forthcoming move to the old factory.

'See you later – and all the best,' he said as he drove off.

In the hall, Gilly found a large group of girls dressed, like herself, in an assortment of T-shirts and shorts. She gave her name to Miss Nesbitt who ticked it off on a list and introduced her to John Hanley, whom Gilly knew was the club's chief coach.

'Hello, Gilly,' he said with a smile. 'Glad you could come along.'

He was a short, muscular man with almost black hair and deep-set dark brown eyes. It was he whom Gilly had to impress most as a promising gymnast.

Marcia came up to her. 'Feeling okay?' she asked. 'Look, there's Anita Douglas, the club's best gymnast. She's going to demonstrate for you.'

Gilly looked across the hall to watch a slender, fair-haired girl circling her shoulders as she warmed up. Gilly had heard about Anita. She was already in the county team and was in line for the regional if not national squad. She had all the characteristics of a star gymnast – ability, bravery, determination and intelligence. I'm going to be like her one day, thought Gilly resolutely.

'Right, girls,' called John Hanley. 'Let's get started.'

The group crowded round him.

'We have to test you,' he explained, 'as so many people want to join Lynx. Therefore we can only admit a few girls who show that they have the makings of being gymnasts. Anita will show you some movements, then we would like you to try them after you have warmed up.'

The girls watched Anita demonstrate movements which would show how much strength, suppleness and sense of balance each girl had. There was another quality, too, which the coaches would expect every budding gymnast to have.

'It's "kinaesthetic awareness",' Marcia explained.

22

'It means knowing where you are in relation to the ground when you are upside down – and in the air.'

After Anita had finished, Miss Nesbitt took the would-be gymnasts through a warm-up session which was like the one that Gilly had seen on her previous visit. Then the girls went through the test movements, watched by Miss Nesbitt and John Hanley who made notes on the performance of each girl.

Once Gilly had seen the movements, she knew that she would have no problems – even walking along the beam. The tests included jumping on the vault springboard, and swinging on the bars as well as trying the splits, cartwheel, handstand, forward and backward rolls and the bridge. In this last movement, the gymnast supports herself on her hands and feet, upside down in an arched position.

Gilly's last test was on the beam. As she went up to it, she looked at Marcia sitting in the back of the hall. Marcia gave her a sharp wink.

Several girls had fallen off the beam but Gilly found her walk along the chamois-covered length of wood and her turn-about much easier than she had expected. She remembered all Marcia's tips and concentrated hard. Thank goodness for those benches, she thought as she jumped off on to the safety mats placed underneath. It was now her turn to wink at Marcia.

After the tests were over, the girls waited tensely for the results. John Hanley and Miss Nesbitt compared notes while they talked together in a corner. Finally, after what seemed hours, the two coaches came forward.

'Girls,' said John Hanley, 'we've decided to take five of you into our novice squad. If you are not one of the five on this occasion, please feel free to come to our next testing session if you would like to have another try. You are also very welcome to apply to join our recreational section.'

This is it, thought Gilly, digging her finger-nails into the palm of her hand. Please, please, please . . .

'Here are the five,' continued John Hanley, 'and would they please come and have a word with me: Stephanie Daley, Gilly Denham, Hazel Henshaw, Shani Patel and Melanie Wood.'

There was a pause, and then someone clapped. Voices sounded, a few with excitement, most with disappointment as they knew that now they had very little chance of becoming serious gymnasts.

Gilly stood still, unable to speak with joy, her mouth wide open. Marcia rushed over to her. 'Well done, Gilly!' she cried, waving her arms with glee.

'It's really thanks to you,' said Gilly, when she was able to produce words. 'I'm so grateful.'

'Nonsense!' shrugged Marcia, 'you've got what gymnastics takes. Anyway, that's just the beginning. From now on, we train together. Wowee!' She dashed away to perform a triumphant back flip.

As the girls who had been tested began to dis-perse, Gilly went up to the coaches. 'That was fun,' she said, still in another world.

Miss Nesbitt gave her a friendly look. 'You weren't too bad, but don't think you were perfect. By the way, you can call me Christine.'

'Yes and you can call me John,' said the chief coach. 'Gilly, with work you might become a gymnast one day. And I mean *work*. You can join us next week – on Tuesday.'

'Gosh, thanks Miss – Christine, thanks John.'

'One thing you must understand, Gilly,' continued John, 'is that if you don't make any progress in the novice squad, then you must leave it.'

Gilly was horrified. 'Of course I'll make progress!'

'That's the spirit,' said Christine with a laugh. 'Now off you go – and we'll see you on Tuesday. Marcia will tell you what kit you need.'

'What will I need?' asked Gilly as she and Marcia left the hall.

'The basics are a club leotard and a sweater and tights for training. You'll also need gymnastics slippers, handguards to protect your hands on the bars and later, a competition leotard. You should think of buying a tracksuit as well. All these things you can buy through the club. And don't forget you've got fees to pay, too.'

'I had forgotten that,' admitted Gilly. 'Tell me what they are.'

'Well, club membership fees and fees to join the BAGA.'

Gilly knew what the BAGA was – the British Amateur Gymnastics Association, the governing body of the sport in Britain. Marcia told her that most gymnasts were enrolled in the BAGA through their clubs so that they could not only be insured but also enter official competitions.

'Oh, there's another item you must get,' added

25

Marcia. 'The club will expect you to keep a diary. You know, to write down everything about learning gymnastics from day to day.'

As they parted, Gilly thanked her friend again for all her help.

'It was nothing – heavens, you'll do *me* a good turn one day, I'm sure.'

At home, however, Gilly met with what at first seemed a setback. While her parents were delighted at her success, they were not very happy about the money they would have to find to enable her to be an active member of Lincston Gymnastics Club.

'Well,' said Mrs Denham with a sigh,' 'you better have an early birthday this year. I do hope it will all be worth it, and not a five-minute wonder.'

'So do I,' said Mr Denham glumly. Just then the telephone rang and he went off to answer it.

Gilly sprang to her feet. 'Mum, I've wanted to be a gymnast for as long as I can remember. I'm certainly not going to give it up now that I've got into a smashing club.'

Mrs Denham put her knitting down. 'I know you will do your best, darling, but it seems to me that you are going to have very little time for other things and I include your school work. Add to that the money we will have to spend on you, and you can see why your father and I are concerned about it.'

Gilly was silent for a moment. Then she spoke, trying to keep her voice level. 'I can find the time; one day I will find the money to pay you back, but I must have your support right now. I'll show you both what I can do and I promise you it will be something to make you proud.'

Her father came back into the room. 'That was a Mr John Hanley of the Lincston Gymnastics Club.' He looked at his daughter. 'He says that you showed excellent promise this afternoon – and he means it. He believes you have every chance of becoming an outstanding member of the club. In the meantime, he has asked us all to the club's disco dance next month.'

Gilly waited for her mother to speak, her eyes wide and shining.

Mrs Denham took up her knitting again with a twinkle in her eye.

'I suppose the most important bit of clothing to get first is your club leotard.'

Gilly ran over to hug her, trying not to cry.

On Tuesday evening, Marcia and her father stopped by the Denham home to pick Gilly up for her first training session. Gilly did not have her leotard yet but her mother had found her a sweater and tights. When they arrived at the hall, Gilly expected that they would begin training straight away. But she had forgotten one thing. Nothing could happen until the equipment was lifted out of store and set up. On her previous visits, the mats, beam and vaulting horse had already been laid out, but now she had to help other members of the novice squad to carry the apparatus into the hall.

'It's a real sweat, this,' grumbled Marcia as they

carted in a large blue crashmat. 'I can't wait until the new building is open.'

But Gilly did not mind at all. She was now a member of the Lincston Gymnastics Club and if she had to lift mats all evening long, she was perfectly happy to do so. After all, it would not be long before the new headquarters was finished.

No one realized then that the conversion of the old factory into a modern gymnastics centre was going to be delayed – deliberately.

Chapter 3

The Lincston Gymnastics Club had taken several years to find premises suitable for their new head-quarters. The ideal centre would be one that was specially built for the sport, both for training and for staging events. But the club's management committee realized that the cost of erecting a new gymnasium and installing modern facilities in it would be far beyond the resources of the club. So the hunt began for an old warehouse, factory or church which could be converted for gymnastics use without too much expense. At the same time, the club's fund-raising group started to hold events to raise the large sum of money needed for buying and converting whatever property became theirs.

'Every month there's something on to get cash in for the new headquarters,' Marcia told Gilly on the bus not long after her test. 'You know, fêtes, jumble sales, sponsored walks – you name it. We even had a sponsored tumble.'

'What's a sponsored tumble?' asked Gilly.

'It's when club members are sponsored on the number of forward rolls, back flips and somersaults they can do. It was very popular.'

'The club disco dance next month – I suppose that will raise some money, too.'

'Indeed it will. We had a square dance last year and that was brill. Packed out, the hall was and we all had a lot of fun – parents as well. And we collected over £300.'

In the spring, the Manton Street factory had come to the club's attention. John Hanley had heard about it by luck because most of the old buildings by the canal had already been knocked down. In the nick of time, John went to the owners and made an offer for the factory. At first, the owners refused to sell it to the club because a local businessman had already said he was interested in the site as a place to build a row of new houses.

'John thought that was that,' explained Marcia. 'But then he got the Borough Council interested in the building as an ideal place for community and recreational use as well as being a gym. So the owners were approached again and the Council came up with a large grant and so eventually the club got their new headquarters.'

'I bet the businessman was cross,' observed Gilly.

'Cross? He went bonkers. He stormed around cursing and waving his arms, trying to get the club to change their mind. But he didn't worry John – or anyone else in the club. We just got on with converting the factory because it was in a dreadful state and there were a billion things to do on it.'

There were, indeed. The factory needed a great deal of repair and conversion work carried out on it before it could be used in comfort for gymnastics and community projects such as a morning nursery school. Not only did items such as broken windows and a leaking roof have to be fixed but also new facilities like a coffee bar and an office had to be installed. Added to that was the essential need to clean and redecorate the whole building. The wires anchoring the vaulting horses and the asymmetrical bars had to have special slots made for them in the floor and a large safety pit had to be dug and constructed.

Not many years ago, safety pits for gymnastics were rare in Britain. These pits are some 2 metres deep and filled with foam rubber so that gymnasts in training can fall into them from apparatus without hurting themselves. This means that gymnasts can learn new moves in the air more quickly and with greater confidence than when practising over a plain wooden floor. When coaches of leading British clubs realized how successful safety pits were in the top gymnastics countries such as the Soviet Union, they began to have them installed in their gymnasiums.

John Hanley realized that acquiring the factory for Lynx's new headquarters gave the club a wonderful chance of having their own pit. So this, too, became a vital part of the conversion programme and one of the most expensive projects.

To save costs, the club decided to undertake a great deal of the conversion work themselves. A works committee was formed under the direction of Mr Galloway, a parent. He recruited volunteer workers from members, coaches and other parents to help with repairs, new construction and decoration.

'My dad's an engineer,' said Gilly. 'I bet he could do something.'

'Well, everyone's welcome to join in. Mr Galloway can find a job down there for anyone of any age. I've been doing some painting, myself. Tell you what, Gilly, I'll take you to Manton Street next weekend. Okay?'

That was fine by Gilly. In the meantime, she could enjoy concentrating on her training.

On her first Tuesday evening, she wore a T-shirt and shorts as the yellow club leotards ordered for the five new novices had not yet arrived. Except for Hazel Henshaw who went to the High with her and Marcia, Gilly was the eldest of the five. Hazel was small and wiry, and never seemed to be afraid of tackling any new move. Stephanie Daley was a dreamy sort of girl who moved gracefully all the time as if she was a dancer. Melanie Wood wore glasses which made her determined to do better than anyone else. Shani Patel, whose family were Indians from Uganda, said very little but she, too, brought a flowing grace and elegance to her movements. 'Ornamental oriental,' said Marcia with a hint of envy.

During that first session, John called the five new novices to him.

'Girls, I want to talk about safety. Every part of your training must be as safe as possible so here are some rules to follow. If you don't follow them, you could quite easily hurt yourself and, what's more important, someone else.'

He looked at each of the girls.

'First, never train if you feel unwell. That's plain common sense, of course. You must also never train unless a qualified coach is present. Serious accidents can happen if you ignore that rule. Understand?'

The five girls nodded.

'Now, on the point of discipline, always pay attention to your coach and never, never play the fool during a training session. Trying to be funny can also lead to accidents, either as a distraction or getting in the way of another gymnast. Let's go on to clothing and things you wear.'

Melanie put her hands to her glasses.

'Yes, Melanie, make sure your glasses are always fastened securely. And on the subject of eyesight, everyone, don't let long hair or anything you wear obstruct your vision.'

Shani, who had long black hair, wrinkled her nose and then grinned.

John continued. 'Don't wear rings, watches or necklaces during training – I'm sure you can see why – and remember that loose clothing can catch on apparatus, as can belts with buckles. Finally, report any injury however small, and keep off training until that injury is better. Any questions?'

'Well,' said Gilly, 'when you think about it, it's amazing that more accidents don't happen in gymnastics.'

John agreed. 'That's exactly why we take safety so seriously. By the way, anyone who doesn't keep to these rules will not last long at this club. Now away you go and get warmed up.'

From her previous visits to the club, Gilly knew about the importance of warming up correctly so that her muscles were prepared for strengthening and suppling exercises. Christine Nesbitt made sure that every joint was exercised during the 20-minute session – from neck down to toes. After the warm-up Gilly felt that she had taken part in a dancing show as all the exercises were performed to lively music.

Christine then explained to the five new novices about the training they were going to do.

'Your aim must be to get into the club's elite

squad because there you get advanced training and the chance to enter important competitions. But first, we've got to get your body ready for learning the skills of gymnastics. You've heard about the three S's – strength, suppleness and stamina – they're the aspects we'll be working hard on so that you can perform moves correctly.'

Stephanie put up her hand. 'Christine, why can't we learn gymnastics moves at the same time?'

'You will learn some, of course, but you must remember that many movements will be strange to your body. So your muscles won't be strong and flexible enough to support your body properly until they have been trained.'

After training had finished and they were helping to put the equipment away, Gilly told Marcia about what she had learned that evening. As well as continuing with more exercises for strength, Christine had given the new novices instruction in correct posture.

'Posture is one of the most important things for all gymnasts to do correctly,' declared Marcia. 'Look at the way the well-known Russian gymnasts stand – straight, tall, and proud. Mind you, it takes an effort at first.'

'It sure does,' said Gilly who had found that standing in the correct position took far more strength than she realized. Christine had placed her in front of a full-length mirror.

'Come on, Gilly, you're a gymnast – not a duck. Feet and legs together, no gaps – stretch up and straighten the spine – pull your shoulder blades together slightly – hold your head up. Not bad, not bad, keep at it.'

Gilly resolved to practise what Christine called her stance every day. Gosh, there were so many points to learn, so many items to remember . . .

'How did it go?' asked Mrs Denham when Gilly arrived home.

'Great, Mum. I must have used every muscle I have.' She slumped in an armchair, feeling tiredness engulf her.

'You probably have, darling. Have some soup – there's some on the cooker – and then a nice bath.'

Gilly would feel tired many times after a gymnastics session in the future, but she would always remember that first training night which made her realize that her whole body had to be in complete physical tune for success.

With Saturday afternoon came Gilly's first visit to the old factory in Manton Street.

'Wear some old clothes,' advised Marcia, 'there's plenty of wet paint about.'

Gilly put on some worn-out jeans and a tattered sweater and got out her bicycle.

'Selling yourself for jumble?' asked her father as he washed the family car.

Gilly stuck out her tongue at him and set off to Market Square where she was to meet Marcia. She found her sitting on her bicycle by the statue of Ebenezer Hodges, mayor of the town over 100 years ago. Marcia offered her a piece of chocolate and led her through the bustling stalls to London Road.

'It's not too far by bike,' said Marcia as she shot off at speed, almost leaving Gilly behind. Away from the town centre, the buildings became older and smaller. Marcia stuck out her left hand and they turned off the main road and coasted down a short hill with terraced houses on either side. Ahead, Gilly could see that several old warehouses were being knocked down. There was an air of dusty desolation about the whole area. The road ended at a low brick wall.

'Gives you the creeps a bit, doesn't it?' called Marcia as she braked to a stop by the last street corner on the left outside a pub called the Narrow Boat.

Narrow Boat?

Strange name, thought Gilly. And then she realized. They were near the canal which long ago had the busy traffic of the canal barges known as narrow boats.

As if reading her thoughts, Marcia said: 'The canal's straight ahead, over the wall. And Manton Street's down here.' She set off around the pub. A boy about Gilly's age with red hair came out of the pub and scowled at her before walking up the hill. Gilly followed Marcia down Manton Street.

Manton Street was only 200 metres long, finishing abruptly at a derelict warehouse. On the left, behind the Narrow Boat pub, was a row of abandoned terrace houses, all due for demolition in the near future. On the right, between Manton Street and the canal, was another old warehouse, still in use with a blue and white sign saying 'Central Car

Spares'. Under the sign was a watchman's cabin which was unmanned. Beyond Central Car Spares was the long, low red brick building which was destined to become the headquarters of the Lincston Gymnastics Club. At the far end of the club building was a small carpark, bounded by the same low brick wall which ran along the canal. In the carpark were half a dozen cars. The entrance to the building was also in the carpark, centred in the middle of the wall. The shabby windows around the single floor of the old factory gave Gilly the impression that this building, too, was scheduled to be destroyed like others in the area. But then she heard the blows of a hammer and the whine of a power drill coming from inside.

'Welcome to our new headquarters,' said Marcia with a bow. She led Gilly through the door into the large space where there was a bustle of people at work with a variety of tools and paint brushes. It was noisy, cold and above all, dirty.

The man with the power drill came over to them. 'Hello, girls,' he cried cheerfully. 'Come to lend a hand?'

'Yes, Mr Galloway,' said Marcia. 'This is Gilly Denham – she's a new member.'

'How do you think you can help us, Gilly?' asked Mr Galloway, indicating the other workers.

'I can paint, too, and sew a bit.'

'Right, then – grab a paintbrush. There'll be some sewing later on, when we start on the curtains.'

For the rest of the afternoon, Gilly and Marcia painted a strip of wall with light yellow emulsion.

Their fellow-volunteers were a mixture of parents and gymnasts, some of whom stood on stepladders so that they could paint the high parts of the wall. There were several other members of the novice squad at work, too. Some parents were painting the thin iron girders which supported the roof – a newer structure than the rest of the building. More were hammering and sewing, while the rest were installing new electrical wiring.

During a halt for a cup of tea, Mr Galloway showed Gilly where some of the new facilities were going to be placed.

'The pit will be dug at the other end of the building,' he explained, 'and at this end we're putting the office, the coffee bar and the changing rooms. Above the office, we're building a balcony for spectators of our events, and over here will be the sound control room – for playing and recording music tapes. As you can see, there's a lot of hard work to be done before we're finished.'

At the end of the afternoon, Gilly came out of the old factory covered with dust and paint but very happy, feeling more than ever that she was a full member of Lynx. Before she and Marcia set off home, she looked over the low wall between the carpark and the canal. The murky water was just below the bottom of the wall and on the other side was the towpath which ran in both directions by yet more industrial buildings. As she and Marcia cycled past Central Car Spares, an old man waved from the watchman's cabin.

'That's Harry,' said Marcia as she waved back.

'He keeps an eye on our building as well, at nights. He's a nice old guy. No one can enter the street without him seeing them.'

For the next two months, she and Marcia went down to the old factory almost every weekend to help with the conversion and in the meantime Gilly learned more about becoming a gymnast at the old hall, gaining confidence with each training session. For the most part, she was conditioning her body in preparation for apparatus work.

One Saturday, as she and Marcia came into the carpark, a man in a green suit and with a bristling black moustache left the building angrily and drove away in a large new red car.

'Who's that?' asked Gilly.

'That's Mr Stanley Culverhay in person. I bet he's tried again to get John to persuade the club to sell the factory to him.'

Marcia was right. It turned out that John could have made a lot of money because Mr Culverhay offered him a large sum if the club would give up their home-to-be. John refused even to discuss the matter and told the surly businessman that he did not want to see him again.

As John had promised, Gilly's parents were asked to the club's disco dance. Mr and Mrs Denham were delighted at Gilly's progress not just as a gymnast but as someone who was getting more self-confident in whatever she did, so they wanted to meet the parents, coaches and gymnasts who were providing their daughter with such a happy and worthwhile interest.

Richard came to the dance, too. The Denhams had asked whether he could so that he would not be alone at home. 'The more, the merrier,' said John.

The dance was held in the old hall which was transformed with coloured lights, flowers, decorations and tables of food prepared by senior members and their parents. Anita Douglas's father acted as resident disc jockey and everyone gyrated and shook to the beat of the loud music. Gilly introduced her family to John, Christine, Mr Cherry and to as many people as she knew. She herself met some members and parents whom she had not seen before.

'Gymnastics? More like a honky tonk,' said Gilly's father with a grin as he shook hands with Mr Galloway.

'I hear you're an engineer,' said Mr Galloway who had plans for Mr Denham. 'We have some central heating problems down at the old factory and I wondered whether you could help . . .' He led Mr Denham off for a chat.

After the winners of the grand raffle were announced – first prize was a hamper of food and wine – Mr Bennett, the club's chairman, told the gathering that they had raised over £500 from the dance. There was a burst of clapping. 'Our next dance,' Mr Bennett went on, 'will be at our new headquarters in Manton Street.' There was even more applause. 'But,' he continued, 'remember that we will still have to keep on raising funds to maintain the new building and buy new equipment.'

As they drove away after the dance, the Denhams were pleased at how the evening had gone.

'Too many girls,' said Richard, 'but the food was good.'

Mrs Denham turned to Gilly. 'I think we are going to enjoy the gym club as much you do.' She had met Mrs Daley before and both mothers had been asked to join the parents' support group which carried out all the many little jobs that arose in the running of the club – jobs such as driving gymnasts to competitions, collecting subscriptions and manning stalls at fêtes.

Mr Denham was flattered that he was asked to help with the Manton Street conversion. 'I'm going down there next week to see what I can do,' he said.

Gilly herself was thrilled with the evening. I'm so lucky, she told herself, all those nice people, a wonderful sport, and soon a fantastic new place to train.

The very next morning, the first blow to many plans happened. Marcia rang up, her voice trembling with shock.

'Gilly, some terrible people have painted words on the front of the old factory – and those words aren't friendly at all!'

Chapter 4

Gilly and Marcia sat in stunned silence in the Moo-Moo milk bar. They were on their way home after inspecting the glaring letters of red paint splattered above the door of the club's new headquarters.

'"Gymnasts get out," indeed!' muttered Gilly. 'That's the last thing Lynx would do.'

'I think it must have been a bunch of kids,' said Marcia, concentrating on a chocolate sundae. 'They would be harder for Harry the watchman to spot than grown-ups.'

'But what kids would want the gym club to go – 'specially as the club has so many young people in it.' Gilly frowned. 'Tell you another thing, Marcia – whoever it was must have known that the entire club was at the disco dance. Usually there's some parent or coach pottering around the building on Saturday night.'

'Well, the club hasn't been exactly silent about the dance – the local paper has been announcing it for weeks,' said Marcia. 'The big question is – what's going to happen now?'

'Hopefully,' said Gilly, 'nothing's going to happen.'

For the next week, it seemed that Gilly was right. The letters of paint were covered up and club life went on as normal. The matter had been reported to the police but as there were no clues to the vandals, no action could be taken. Work on the factory was progressing so well that a date for the official opening had been fixed for the end of term – now just a month away. The club had enlisted the services of a professional builder to speed the conversion work and the main tasks were nearly finished.

But to the dismay of the entire club, the vandals struck again. Gilly and Marcia were about to go home after Tuesday training in the old hall when

Inspector Graham of the Lincston police walked in to talk with John.

Out of the corner of her eye, Gilly could see John's face fall in disbelief. Bad news, she thought.

Bad news, it was. A police patrol had discovered that the end windows by the main door had been smashed sometime in the early evening after sunset.

'Apparently,' Gilly told her mother later, 'no one saw or heard anything, even though there's a night watchman bang next door.'

'The whole matter is very worrying,' said Mrs Denham, 'and I'm convinced other parents must think the same. Those crazy people could start attacking Lynx gymnasts next.'

'It won't get as bad as that, Mum, surely not,' said Gilly. But she shivered all the same.

The next day, Marcia brought further news to the High School – news she had heard from her father. 'John rang Dad and told him that the police think some boys are responsible. It seems the boys live nearby and go about in a kind of gang.'

'The only boy I've seen around there is that red-headed one who has something to do with the Narrow Boat pub.'

'Yeah,' said Marcia, 'I know who you mean, that boy who looks cross all the time.'

'What are the police actually going to do about it?' asked Gilly.

'Give the boys a good talking to, I expect. But so far, there's nothing that actually links the boys with the damage.'

'Doesn't anyone suspect Harry?'

'Harry? Of course not. Everyone in Lincston knows him – he's an old soldier and completely trustworthy. He wouldn't have his job if he wasn't. Besides, he has a gammy leg and can't move very fast.'

It was all very mysterious.

For a while after that, the old factory was left in peace. The windows were replaced and the conversion work entered its last stage.

At the Church Hall, the new novices continued with their body preparation. They now wore the yellow leotards of Lynx with considerable pride. During each period of training, Christine gave the girls exercises which, though tiring at first, became easier to perform as their bodies became stronger and more supple. Christine was particularly anxious that the girls acquired strong feet and ankles.

'They're probably the most common area for injury,' she told the squad. 'They're expected to support a body flying from a height to land on unfamiliar floor surfaces and not to suffer any discomfort at all. They will suffer, of course, if they're not prepared.'

So Gilly and her friends carried out many exercises to strengthen feet, ankles and legs, and several of the exercises were the kind used by ballet dancers.

'Darling,' said Mrs Denham, 'I do hope that you are not going to end up with short, ugly leg muscles however strong they are.'

Gilly laughed. 'No, I certainly won't. Christine makes sure that our leg muscles are stretched as well as strengthened so that they always remain long. That's very important for both gymnasts and ballet dancers.'

The novice girls also learned exercises to strengthen the stomach, lower back, chest and shoulder girdle.

'We even have exercises to make our arms, wrists and hands stronger,' Gilly told her mother. 'That makes sense, because in many moves your arms take the place of your legs.'

'I don't quite follow you, Gilly.'

'Oh Mum, in moves like handstands and cart-wheels. See?'

It was about this time that Gilly began to find out that she was making excellent progress in her body conditioning. She had the advantage of being more supple than her friends and her splits were far better than those of the others. But her progress and growing popularity in Lynx gave rise to something she had not bargained for – jealousy.

In the other section of the novice squad, the best gymnast was a girl with dark hair and high cheekbones called Caroline Mayhew. However, Caroline had one serious fault; she was a bad loser. When she saw how well Gilly was developing as a gymnast, she took a sudden dislike to her. Before long, Caroline would not talk to Gilly or even look at her. Several times, Gilly tried to be friendly, but on each occasion Caroline turned and walked haughtily away.

'I don't think she's worth worrying about,' said Stephanie to Gilly one evening when training had finished. 'Stuck up prig, she is.'

47

Gilly shrugged and wondered why Caroline hated her. But soon her good spirits stopped her from feeling hurt at Caroline's snubs and she thought no more about it.

She had almost forgotten about the vandals when the worst damage yet was discovered at the Manton Street building a fortnight later. The main door was forced open and equipment and fittings in the gymnasium were either broken, slashed or daubed with paint. Among the breakages, a vaulting horse was wrecked, the wires on the asymmetric bars cut and a crash mat ripped open. Several tools were stolen, as were two track suits belonging to a couple of coaches.

'We're not going to be able to open in *three* months, let alone one,' said Mr Galloway in despair as he inspected the devastation. Many club members and their parents wept when they saw how much of their hard work had been in vain. The opening of the new headquarters had to be postponed until further notice.

This time, the story of the vandalism appeared in the Lincston Advertiser together with photographs. As a result, the club received much sympathy and many offers of help such as money and fittings, but the extra work which now had to be carried out still meant that no date could be fixed for the opening in the near future.

More and more parents became worried about the situation. A group, led by Mr Henshaw, suggested to John and Mr Bennett that a security patrol be hired to check the factory every night.

'We can't possibly afford it,' John told them. 'And in any case, the police check the area frequently and there's a night watchman close by.'

'He must be absolutely useless,' retorted Mr Henshaw. 'And what, may I ask, are the police doing about it?'

The Lincston police were, in fact, baffled. Ever since the first act of vandalism had been reported to them, they had regularly visited Manton Street by day and by night. The main mystery was that all the damage had been done at a time when Harry had been on duty at the next-door Central Car Spares depot. The old watchman and Sid, his occasional relief, were familiar to nearly every police officer in the town. But so far, neither Harry nor Sid had seen or heard any strangers come into Manton Street on foot or by car.

However, the police were almost convinced that the culprits were the gang of boys who lived in the neighbourhood. As soon as the break-in was reported, a police car sped to the area and the boys were interviewed in the presence of their parents. Each boy hotly denied having anything to do with the damage at the new gymnasium and once again there were no clues to show who the vandals were. All the police could do was to give a warning to the gang to stay well clear of Manton Street – a warning resented by the boys and their parents.

'We can't do anything else until we get a bit of luck,' said Inspector Graham to John. 'Like someone being spotted up to no good at the building, or something left behind that could give us a lead.'

John realized how difficult the problem was, but he asked everyone connected with the club to be on the lookout for anything suspicious.

Gilly had been thinking hard about the whole situation. 'I'd like to know more about the boys,' she said to Marcia. 'Let's go and talk to Harry.'

Early the next evening, having placed lights on their bicycles, the two girls coasted up to the Central Car Spares warehouse. Harry let them squeeze into his little cabin, which was cosy and warm with an electric kettle, a radio and a telephone. He was a short man, almost bald except for wisps of white hair.

'What can I do for you, ladies?' he asked after they had accepted a mug of steaming tea.

'We're sort of playing detectives,' said Gilly carefully.

'What, you too?' The old man snorted. 'I've had enough questions from the police. I tell them I ain't seen nothing.'

'What about the boys, Harry?' asked Marcia, sipping her tea.

'What about the boys, indeed? They ain't done nothing either. I've known Sean since he was a nipper. If you think it's the boys what done it, then away you go.'

'We don't think that at all,' said Gilly, 'because there's no proof. But tell us about Sean.'

'You know Sean O'Connor. Red-headed lad – his old man runs the pub over there.'

Gilly remembered the red-haired boy she had

seen on her first visit to Manton Street. She also remembered the scowl on the boy's face.

'Sean's a good one – I'm telling you,' continued Harry. 'He's clever, too – he's doing well at school. And he keeps the other lads out of mischief.'

'What do you mean?' asked Gilly.

'Well, he gets them to play games together, for one thing – you know, football, cricket. And he thought up the Manton Street party. Lovely, that was.' The old man smiled at the memory. 'That was last summer. Everyone come from all around here. Those boys was putting up tables and flags and balloons. There was games. There was grub, there was drink, and there was dancing. A great time was had by all.'

Marcia and Gilly looked at each other. That's a smashing idea, thought Gilly. Maybe the gym club could do the same, sometime . . .

'Yep,' nodded Harry, 'those lads is good ones.'

When they had finished their tea, the girls thanked the old watchman and left for home.

'I'd like to meet the Manton gang,' said Gilly as they cycled up London Road. 'They don't sound too bad.'

'I'm not sure,' replied Marcia. 'You know what boys can be like. Well, Harry certainly thinks they're all right. But we're no nearer to finding out who wrecked our new gym.'

That evening, Gilly sat thoughtfully in the kitchen. Her father was placing an ice tray in the refrigerator. He had helped to install some heating units at the old factory and was as upset as anybody at the senseless damage done to them.

'What's on your mind?' he asked, closing the refrigerator door.

'Nothing really, Dad. I'm just wondering what can be done to protect the new gym.'

Mr Denham thought for a moment. 'Apart from mounting a 24-hour guard, there's nothing much anyone can do – particularly as Manton Street is now so empty and deserted. As I say, you've got to check the building the whole time, and who's going to do that?'

By next morning, Gilly had an answer, or rather, an idea. Just before the next training session at the gym club, she took her four fellow-novices and Marcia into a corner of the hall.

'Look,' she said earnestly, 'I think we can do something about keeping an eye on the Manton Street gym.'

'Like what?' asked Hazel.

'Like forming a small group to check on the factory at odd times after school and at weekends.'

'But the wreckers always come out at night,' observed Melanie.

'I know,' said Gilly. 'But whoever-it-is might come and spy on the building in the daylight. We know that our coaches have jobs during the day and that the police can't be there the whole time either. All we need do is look out for anyone or anything odd – just by popping down there in turns every afternoon. It's better than doing nothing.'

Marcia clapped her hands. 'It's a smashing idea, Gilly. Count me in!'

'And me!' cried Stephanie excitedly.

The others agreed enthusiastically. 'You never know, we could spot something important,' declared Hazel.

'Exactly,' said Gilly. 'Now how about this for a name – a name for our group . . .'

By the time training began, the High Flyers patrol had been born – and organized. Each High Flyer was going to try and visit Manton Street at least one afternoon a week. After every visit, each girl would report to Gilly on what they saw, if anything, and Gilly would make a note in a diary. 'We should go in pairs whenever possible,' she said. So it was arranged that Shani and Melanie would go to the area the following afternoon after school.

Training that evening continued with strengthening and suppling exercises. The novices had been performing these two types of exercise together for some time.

'Suppleness has two aspects,' Christine had told them. 'It gives you a good range of movement in the joints and ensures that your muscle tendons are flexible for many moves. In other words, a supple gymnast is not a stiff gymnast.'

Gilly was lucky in that she was fairly supple in the hip and shoulder joints; indeed, she had been tested for this when she joined Lynx. But she had to work hard at suppling her ankles and wrists as well as her legs, back, tummy and thighs. For most of the novice squad, suppling exercises were a major reason why becoming a good gymnast took a great deal of effort.

After some stretching exercises, Christine announced that the novices would start working to pass the basic proficiency scheme of the British Amateur Gymnastics Association. The scheme had four awards – or stages – and each had ten tests on different moves. The easiest award was Award 4 and the hardest Award 1, and in each, six tests had to be achieved to gain a pass.

Christine also told the girls that each novice had to obtain Award 1 to be considered for the club's elite squad.

Well, that's something to work for, thought Gilly, and something I'm going to get.

Later that evening, Christine introduced the girls to dive rolls as a basic preparation for working on floor and vault. On floor, she made them pretend they were diving over a barrel to perform a forward roll. But for vaulting, they had to make a short run, jump off the springboard and roll on a crash mat.

Gilly was elated. 'It's wonderful fun!' she told her mother when she got home. 'It helps you get used to different parts of vaulting.'

Mrs Denham smiled anxiously. 'I'd rather you didn't perform dive rolls in here,' she said as she steered a coffee table out of her daughter's way.

Two afternoons later, Gilly and Marcia went down to the old factory in their roles as High Flyers. It had been raining and the sky was dark and dull. As usual, Manton Street was deserted and silent. Ghost town, thought Gilly as she looked around the car-park. 'Things seem okay,' she said. 'Let's go get a milkshake.'

The girls had a last look over the canal wall. The water had risen with the rain. 'Hope we don't get flooded as well,' said Gilly as she watched a plastic bottle drift by.

Just then they heard several running footsteps behind them. They spun around to face five tough-looking boys bearing down on them. Gilly recognized one as the red-headed Sean from the Narrow Boat pub.

'Let me go!' cried Marcia as the boys seized the girls by the arms.

'No nonsense, now!' snapped Sean. 'We're all going to have a little chat. Bring them along, lads!'

The girls, their hearts beating rapidly, were dragged quickly across the street into one of the abandoned houses opposite the factory.

Chapter 5

The house into which Gilly and Marcia had been taken was fast becoming a ruin. Like its neighbours in the row, the windows were boarded up, but somehow the boys had managed to open the front door. Inside, there was just enough light to see peeling wallpaper, bare floorboards, and a pile of old newspapers and circulars by the broken stairs. Gilly smelt dust and damp and tried to stifle her growing feeling of fear.

Marcia was still protesting. 'You clumsy great oxes, just leave go!'

The boys pushed them through to a back room. Someone opened another boarded window and at last it was light enough for the girls to see and study their captors.

Sean O'Connor they knew by sight, but the other four boys were strangers. Of the two holding Gilly, one had striking blond hair and the other was very short in height, even shorter than she was. One of the boys grasping Marcia had tousled dark hair while the other was extremely tall.

Marcia tried again. 'For heaven's sake, push off, you – '

'Shut up!' Sean glared at her. 'Okay, put them against the wall and let go of their arms.'

Gilly wondered what was going to happen next. She decided quickly that the best thing to do was to start talking as naturally as she could.

'Sean, why have you brought us here?' she asked.

Sean's scowl quickly switched to her. 'How did you know my name?'

'Harry told us. He also said that you boys were a good lot. That's why I'm surprised you've treated us like crooks in a TV film.'

Sean blinked his eyes in surprise and his friends

looked at each other in amazement. This was clearly an unexpected beginning to their scheme.

'So,' Gilly went on, 'what can we do for you?'

The tall boy broke in. 'You think we've smashed up your building!'

'I don't think anything of the kind,' said Gilly.

'Nor do I,' declared Marcia. 'There's no proof, for starters.'

'Belt up!' said Sean aggressively. 'Like Titch says, a lot of people in this town do think we're to blame, and they include the police. Let me tell you something: before you gym crowd came, this was our neck of the woods. We used to play indoor football in that old factory and we kept nice and dry when it rained.'

'That's right,' said the blond-headed boy, 'really good it was. Now look at it.'

Sean nodded. 'As Rob says, it was a great place. But now – but now we can't use it at all. As soon as your club bought the factory, that was us out in the cold. Yes, you have the right to keep anyone you choose out of your own property and we can accept that. But what we can't stand, and won't stand, is the way we've been put on the line by the police for the damage done to the building.'

Tousle-Hair spoke up. 'You say we've treated you like crooks, but wait till you've had the police in your house, their cars parked outside for all the neighbours to see. We can't go anywhere around here now without people whispering and pointing at us.'

'Okay,' said Gilly, her confidence returning, 'I

58

can understand how you feel. But I can also understand why the police are interested in you – it's their
job to look for clues everywhere. But what can
Marcia and I do to make the situation better?'

Sean turned to her. 'We're getting hassled by the
fuzz, right? Now we don't want to be the only
people in the firing line, so we want you and your
gym pals to know that we can do a bit of hassling,
too.'

'What do you mean?' asked Gilly.

'I mean that every now and then we are going to
cause a little bit of bother to you gymnasts – like
bringing you in here.'

'I don't believe you,' said Marcia, getting cross. 'I
never expected you to be bully boys, not after what
Harry said. And I bet Gilly thinks the same.'

Gilly agreed. 'Sean, that's going to get you
nowhere. The people who think you've got something to do with the breakages at the factory will be
even more convinced that you have. Things will get
worse for you, not better.'

'Well, what are we to do?' asked the small boy.
The girls learned later that he was called Lofty,
although his real name was Michael.

Gilly thought hard. The novice group had formed
the High Flyers to patrol the area . . . She suddenly
had the answer.

'Listen,' she said. 'When our gym club has moved
here, it's going to grow larger. It's not going to be
just for girl gymnasts from other parts of the town,
it's going to be open to folk around here.'

The boys were immediately interested and listened intently.

'I'll tell you another thing,' Gilly went on. 'Several parents in Lynx want to start a boys' section, my parents among them, because my brother Richard would like to have a go at gymnastics.'

Sean interrupted her. 'You think we could join?' he asked, trying to sound casual but not succeeding in hiding his curiosity.

'If there's a boys' section,' she said slowly, 'and if you're good enough. But you'll be banned from applying if you've upset members of the club.'

'Your people don't like us whatever we do,' said Rob wistfully. 'We'll never get near your old club.'

'I think you can do something about it,' said Gilly. 'Let me tell you about our High Flyers.' She explained how their group of six novices was organized to patrol near the factory on the look out for anything strange.

'That's not a bad idea,' said Lofty.

Sean knew what Gilly was going to say next. 'You reckon we could do the same thing – start a patrol.'

'Yes, you could,' Gilly told them, 'and once people knew you were keeping an eye on the new headquarters, they wouldn't think you were involved in causing the mess there. Also, I could then say to John Hanley – he's our chief coach – that all of you should have the chance of becoming members.'

The boys waited for Sean to speak.

'All right,' he said after a pause, 'we'll think about it.'

'Let me know what you decide,' said Gilly. She gave Sean her telephone number.

'Sorry if we were a bit rough,' the tousled-haired Pete said to Marcia as he led the way out of the derelict house.

Marcia, who had a large smudge of dirt on her face, was still none too happy with her experience. 'If you lot dare to jump on us again, we'll have you hounded out of Lincston!' she cried.

The boys laughed and Gilly tried not to smile.

'See you around,' said Lofty as the girls cycled off.

Up in the town, they stopped to have the milk-shakes they had promised themselves.

Marcia shook her head when they sat down at a table. 'You were amazing, Gilly,' she said, 'you got those boys right on our side. I was too scared to think straight in that grotty dump.'

'We don't know yet if they'll agree,' said Gilly, looking into her chocolate milkshake. 'They may decide a patrol is a big waste of time – 'specially as they have a bad reputation to live down.'

But later that night, the phone rang just before Gilly went to bed. Richard answered it. 'Gilly, it's for you,' he called, puzzled. 'Someone's ringing from a party.'

Gilly was confused at first when she took the phone. There were certainly sounds of happy voices and clinking glasses. 'Hello?' she said, hesitantly.

'It's me, Sean. Just to say we've decided to help you. We're now the Manton Mobsters – fighting fit and ready for duty.'

'That's great, Sean,' Gilly was delighted. 'Now we can cover the Manton Street neighbourhood really well.'

Sean and she decided that the boys should patrol around the last thing at night and in the early morning. At other times, the High Flyers and other gym club people were likely to be visiting or working in the area.

Before she said goodnight, Gilly explained to her family that Sean was 'phoning from the saloon bar of the Narrow Boat pub where he lived and not from a party.

'Lucky girl,' said Richard, 'fancy having a boy friend who lives in a pub. Ow!' he cried as his sister thumped him.

From then on, Manton Street was patrolled regularly by the High Flyers and the Mobsters. The gymnasts and the boys could not watch the street the whole time, of course, but their scouting cut down the opportunities for anyone to wreck the factory without being seen. There were no further signs of vandalism at the club's new headquarters and the work of repairing the previous damage went ahead. However, the club's management committee decided this time not to fix a date for the official opening until all the work had been completed.

Meanwhile, the new novices continued with their training. Christine had talked to them about stamina and how important it was for gymnasts to have bodies fit and capable of going through a long training session or a strenuous competition without feeling too tired. So frequently, the novices had to go through a programme of repeating exercises quickly, one after another. They also had to skip with ropes and go for runs. Gilly enjoyed this and made sure that she skipped and ran at home at least once a week.

Christine was anxious at the same time not to make the girls train too hard at each session. She told them: 'Training must be gradual, otherwise it puts a lot of strain on your body.'

Another aspect of keeping fit was diet. Gilly learned that if she neglected her diet, her performance could be affected by lack of energy and weight problems. Eating a well-balanced diet meant that her body would receive the right amounts of nutrients, the parts of food vital for good health. Nutrients, she was told, are classified as proteins, fats, carbohydrates, vitamins, minerals and water.

Gilly had heard about calories, the measurement of energy that food provides, but she did not know that if she did not eat enough calories, she would be down on energy and lose weight. A girl of her build taking part in gymnastics needed at least 2000 calories a day.

She wrote in her training diary: *The main nutrients supplying energy are carbohydrates, proteins and fats, carbohydrates being the main source. Carbohydrates are the starches and sugars found in foods such as fruits, breads, vegetables, cakes and biscuits. Fats are plentiful in cheese, cream, butter, salad oils, bacon and nuts. Protein is supplied by meat, fish, milk, cheese, nuts and eggs and I need at least three*

63

of these foods every day. However, she was aware from her mother that she should not eat too much animal protein and fat.

Gilly could now perform a first-class handstand. Christine had insisted that all the novices should concentrate on perfecting this basic gymnastics move. She was pleased with Gilly's style and used her to show other gymnasts how the handstand should be done.

'The handstand,' said Christine at one demonstration, 'should show a perfectly straight line from hands to feet. See how Gilly is squeezing the muscles of her backside tightly together and sucking in her tummy muscles while extending fully in her shoulders. That, girls, is the secret of a good handstand.'

What was not a secret was the jealousy shown by Caroline Mayhew when Gilly was picked out by Christine because she had completed a move or an exercise faultlessly. Caroline was making good progress herself but she could not bear being bettered by someone who had joined the gym club after her.

It did not take long for Marcia, too, to upset Caroline. 'What are you looking so glum-faced about, then?' she asked Caroline one evening after Gilly had executed an excellent dive roll over the vaulting horse.

'Shove off,' snapped Caroline, tossing her head as she turned her back on the vaulting.

'I can't understand that girl,' said Marcia to Gilly later. 'She has absolutely no reason to hate you – or anyone else in the club, for that matter. Bet you anything that she'll come a cropper sometime. By the way, what's news from the Mobsters?'

There was no news at all. The boys had phoned their patrol reports in to Gilly regularly and not once had they seen anything suspicious during the time they had been watching the factory. Gilly was still sure that their patrolling was helping to keep the vandals away. She now needed to tell John about the Mobsters and how helpful they were being to the gym club. John had announced that a boys' section was going to be formed definitely once the conversion work was finished, and she wanted to suggest the Mobsters should be considered for membership. She decided to tackle John on a Saturday afternoon when he and several club people would be busy painting and decorating down at Manton Street.

Sean now trusted Gilly and her friends fully. One day, over a bag of crisps which he had brought from the Narrow Boat, he confided to Gilly that he wanted to become a sportswriter for a newspaper after he had finished with school and that he was interested in all kinds of sport.

'Well,' said Gilly, munching away, 'you've now got the chance of learning something about the best sport in the world – 'specially as you have a club on your doorstep.' She could not tell him that he should try and look more cheerful; his scowl seemed to be fixed for ever on his face.

On the night before Gilly was going to speak to

John about Sean and his gang, all her good intentions received another shock.

As John was locking up the factory late that evening before going home, he was knocked out by an unknown assailant.

Chapter 6

The night when John Hanley was attacked at the factory was not only windy but pitch black. There were no street lamps at the end of Manton Street, and the carpark was always in darkness unless lights were on in the building. So when John came out of the door, he could not see or hear anyone.

'Whoever it was crept up behind me when I was busy with the keys,' he said later, rubbing the back of his head where he had been hit with some kind of club. Fortunately the blow was not severe and he recovered consciousness within a few moments to find himself lying by the front step. He pushed himself to his feet and staggered off to Harry's cabin to raise the alarm.

The police came around in a rush, sirens shrieking and blue lamps flashing on their cars. Once again, there was nothing to see in the vicinity of the factory, and once again Harry had not noticed anyone entering Manton Street. The only car left in the carpark was John's and it seemed likely that his attacker – or attackers – had hidden behind it undetected.

Inspector Graham drove John up to the town's hospital for treatment to a deep cut on his head and for a check-up. The hospital staff made John spend the night there for observation and let him go the following afternoon. In the meantime, the police combed the area searching for clues. To the annoyance of the Mobsters, police officers questioned them yet again. But this time, few people believed that the boys had anything to do with the attack.

The news of the assault spread quickly through the gym club. When Marcia and her father stopped by the next afternoon to take Gilly in their car to the factory, their faces were long with worry. Mrs Denham asked them in for a cup of tea.

'The situation's very serious,' said Mr Cherry. 'A meeting of parents is being held tonight and I gather that a proposal is being made to close down the gym club.'

Gilly was aghast. 'That's impossible!' she cried.

'No, darling, it's not,' said her mother. 'Vandalism is one thing but physical injury is another. I can quite understand how these parents feel and I shall be going along to the meeting myself.'

'Why don't we buy another headquarters instead of Manton Street?' asked Marcia. 'Surely that would be better than bringing the club to an end.'

'I'm afraid we can't do that,' explained Mr Cherry. 'Lynx has put a lot of hard-earned money into the Manton Street project and if the building is sold now as an uncompleted gymnasium, much of that money will be lost. The building was a bargain in the first place and only a miracle could produce another place like it in Lincston which the club could afford.'

'Then Lynx better stay at the Church Hall,' declared Gilly.

'No, that idea won't work either,' said Mr Cherry. 'The club has to move from there in a couple of months. Then the hall will be turned into a social club for old people.'

'Surely there's something we can do,' pleaded Gilly, her eyes flashing. 'It can't mean the end of the gym club.'

'Unfortunately, with parents in their present mood,' said Mr Cherry, 'it could mean just that.'

Later that afternoon, Gilly put down the bright red curtain she was sewing at Manton Street and slipped off to see Sean. She knocked on the back door of the Narrow Boat. Mrs O'Connor, a large and ample woman, was far from pleased to see her. 'You again,' she greeted Gilly grumpily. 'We had the police around again last night. When's it going to stop?'

Sean appeared behind her. 'It's okay, Mum – even they said we couldn't have slugged that gym club bloke. What's going on, Gilly?'

In the kitchen, Gilly told him about the concern of the gym club parents over the attack on John and how the existence of the club was threatened.

'Well,' said Sean slowly, 'if that happens, everything would have been a flipping great waste of time – our patrolling and all. So we'll pack it in, eh?'

'No!' said Gilly firmly, 'that's just what we are not going to do. Whatever the parents decide tonight, we've got to keep watching the factory. Some day, some time, those wreckers will make a big mistake. And we've got to be around when they do.'

'I wish I was as hopeful as you are,' said Sean. 'But let's first see what happens at the meeting before we make up our minds what to do next. I don't want to let you down but I don't want to waste time and energy if there's no point to it.'

As Gilly went back to her sewing, she was determined, with or without the boys, that she was going to find out who was intent on driving the Lincston Gymnastics Club away.

'Tonight's going to be a real cliff-hanger,' said Mr Cherry as he and Marcia dropped Gilly off at her home. 'Here's hoping the club will survive.'

'It must, Dad, it must,' said Marcia, trying to keep the worry out of her voice.

Here's hoping, thought Gilly, waving to her friends as they drove off.

Both Mr and Mrs Denham went to the meeting at the Church Hall and Gilly had to wait impatiently at home all evening until they returned, before she heard what happened.

Her mother told her that there was a large crowd of parents facing the club's management committee which was led by Mr Bennett, the chairman. Many of the parents were obviously upset about the vandalism and attack on John Hanley at the Manton Street building. John himself appeared, with a bandage around his head, and received a welcome burst of applause.

Mr Bennett described the damage done so far at the new headquarters and the attack on John. He said the meeting was held by request so that all parents connected with the club could ask questions about the situation or let other club people know what they felt about it.

After that, several parents asked questions about the security of the factory and the answer was basically the same: while the police had been increasing their checks on the area, there was still no indication of who was dead set on persecuting the club.

Then Mr Hobday stood up to speak. Gilly knew that he had a loud voice and was used to getting his own way.

That evening, Mr Hobday said that he was speaking for a group of parents who believed Lincston Gymnastics Club should either give up Manton Street or close down. He said it was clear that the club had enemies among the local inhabitants who did not want strangers in their neighbourhood. If these enemies were determined enough to cause violence as well as vandalism, then there was a great risk of danger to every member of the club, whatever age. The brutal attack on John, in his opinion, emphasized that the new headquarters would never be a place safe enough to use without fear. Whatever other parents decided to do, he for one was going to take his daughter Lynn away from the club. Several parents clapped in agreement.

After Mr Hobday had sat down, Mrs Tatlow got to her feet. Her daughter Veronica was one of the most experienced gymnasts in the club and a member of the senior team.

Mrs Tatlow said that Mr Hobday was absolutely right and she wanted to propose that Lincston Gymnastics Club be disbanded immediately.

Mr Bennett announced that the proposal would be put to the vote for the committee to consider, but first, would anyone like to speak against it?

No one spoke for a moment, and Mrs Denham began to think that the club had lost the support it need to stay alive. Then someone cleared his throat.

'Yes,' said Mr Cherry quietly, 'I would like to speak.'

Mr Cherry reminded everyone that Lincston produced gymnasts who were well-known for their high standards of performance and for their courage in taking on a sport which had elements of danger. It seemed to him that the club would be letting its young members down totally if their leaders, their parents, their coaches could not show that they, too, had guts – guts to stand up against the criminals who were trying to destroy the results of the hard work and dedication which so many had contributed for so many years.

'It was powerful stuff, listening to it,' Mrs Denham told Gilly, 'and he had everyone's attention.'

Mr Cherry went on to say that the situation at Manton Street could not go on for ever. Sooner or later, it would end in the club's favour – and it could be sooner if every parent and member gave wholehearted support to the management committee who were doing a splendid job. Nothing and no one was going to scare him away, even if he had to camp every night in the Manton Street carpark. So he certainly wasn't going to be timid and vote to end an organization that was extra special and worthwhile for young people.

Mr Cherry not only received more applause than Mr Hobday but also some cheers as well.

'We knew then,' said Mrs Denham, 'that the club was going to stay alive, vote or no vote.'

When Mr Bennett asked for a show of hands for Mrs Tatlow's proposal, only a few were raised. Mr Cherry had won the day.

Afterwards, a committee of parents and club officers were elected to come up with ideas on how to safeguard the factory so that it could have its official opening as soon as possible. Mr Denham became one of its members.

'You'll have to have a uniform and a helmet and be a guard, Dad,' said Gilly with a smile.

'I hope the vandals won't force us to do that,' observed her father. 'But it will be very difficult to think of any other way to protect the building.'

But despite the formation of the watchdog committee, several parents including Mr Hobday and Mrs Tatlow withdrew their daughters from membership of the club.

Later, Gilly phoned Sean to tell him that the club was safe, certainly for the time being. He was delighted. 'The Mobsters will be out on patrol as usual and I bet we'll spot something eventually,' he told Gilly confidently.

Before the following Tuesday night's training began at the hall, Gilly and her friends gathered to talk about the meeting.

'I hear your dad was fantastic,' said Hazel to Marcia.

'He's certainly never made a speech like that before,' replied Marcia proudly.

'Oh my,' said Shani, 'if only he could speak to the bad people . . .'

'We've got to find them first,' said Gilly, wondering if that was ever going to happen.

All the girls knew, however, that even though most parents were still giving their support to the club, there was a limit to the patience, time and money which was being spent on the effects of the vandalism. Another really serious set-back at the factory would lose that parental support and make the closure of the club almost certain.

'Right, girls – let's have our warm-up,' called Christine.

The music started and the girls began their usual 20-minute period of warming up followed by strengthening and suppling exercises. Christine then announced some surprise news.

'I want to hold a novice floor and vault competition before long,' she told the squad. 'But only those of you who have passed Award 1 of the BAGA Awards can take part.'

Gilly had already taken the first three awards. She had found Award 4 and Award 3 fairly easy and achieved passes for all the tests she attempted. In Award 2, the movements were harder. For example, she had to learn how to do a backward roll which ended in a handstand. Another movement, which was more difficult than it looked, was to perform two cartwheels one after another in a straight line. However, Gilly got through the award without meeting any serious problems. After Award 2 came Award 1, and that was the hard one, with movements such as the back flip and forward handspring. Gilly had known that she would find this award difficult to pass, especially as she could not yet perform a satisfactory back flip.

'You'll be flapping your arms and learning how to fly next,' said her father when he met her after training one Saturday morning not long after.

Gilly laughed. 'Sometimes it does feel like flying, 'specially when you're vaulting.'

She and Marcia were off to Manton Street for the afternoon. Marcia was helping to tile the wall in the little kitchen and Gilly was sewing another of the red curtains which were going up in the club office. As usual, there were several gymnasts and their parents at work and there was a sense of excitement everywhere as the finishing touches to the building were nearing completion.

'How could people ever consider closing the gym club,' said Gilly to Melanie who was also working on a curtain.

'If there's danger about, of course they would,' said Melanie, trying to thread a needle. 'I hear Mr Galloway is trying to get the Council to put up some street lamps so it won't be so dark around here. I hope he succeeds because this part of the world gives me the willies.'

The club's watch-dog committee had taken other precautions, too. As soon as darkness fell, all the young gymnasts working in the new headquarters were asked to go home, unless they were with a parent. On that day, nearly everyone left together.

Gilly was one of the last to leave, as she wanted to finish the hem of her curtain. When she came out into the carpark, a voice called from the darkness.

'Hi, Gilly!'

It was Titch, the tall boy, on patrol with his fellow Mobster Pete. Gilly stopped for a chat.

'How's it going?' she asked.

Titch shook his head. 'Haven't seen nothing. We're going home.'

He told her that they had checked the whole street and that there was no one about.

While Gilly was telling the boys about the plan for street lamps, a girl came out of the old building and pushed past them. The girl turned to look at Gilly who recognized her in the light from a window.

'Good night, Caroline,' she said.

Caroline sniffed and stumped away without a word.

'Friendly soul,' observed Bert.

'She's always like that,' Gilly told them. 'She doesn't like me at all.'

After she had informed the boys that she was definitely going to talk to John Hanley about their gym club membership, Gilly herself left for home. She was still thankful that the club had not been closed and with the opening of the new gym surely not far away, it was time that John was made aware of the five Mobsters and the efforts they were making for the club.

However, the next afternoon brought the Denham family a major shock when a surprise visitor arrived. It was Christine, who was clearly distressed and almost crying.

Mr Denham sat her down in an armchair while Gilly brought her a cup of coffee.

'What on earth is the matter?' asked Mrs Denham.

'I just don't know how to tell you,' said Christine, her voice shaking. 'Those awful vandals have painted words on the new headquarters again. But that's not all.' She turned to Gilly.

'What do you mean?' Gilly suddenly felt cold.

Christine controlled herself and sat up straight. 'Gilly, people are saying that you had a hand in this latest outrage!'

Chapter 7

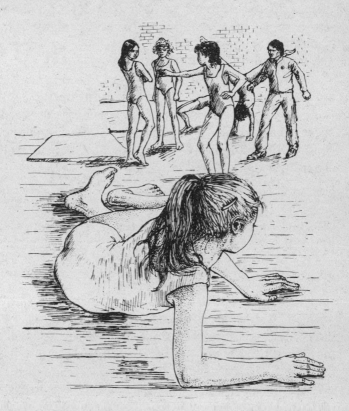

The Denham family were stunned. What, Gilly having something to do with covering the factory wall with smears of paints?

'It's utter nonsense, of course,' said Mr Denham to Christine, 'but perhaps you would tell us about it.' He gave Gilly a protective hug.

Gilly herself felt as if someone had stuck a knife in her. How could this happen to her, Gilly, after she had tried so hard to help the club. Then she grew angry at the thought of being blamed for something she had not done. 'Yes, Christine, please tell us about it,' she said firmly.

Christine told them that early in the morning the police had discovered the fresh graffiti on the same wall by the door as before. Once again, the words were splashed on in red paint, but this time they were splattered many times over the entire wall. There were just two words used:

GIRLS GO

But on the bottom of the wall on the right, scrawled just once, was another message:

BOYS STAY

This made the police think again immediately of the boys in the Manton Street area. As a result, two boys were now under suspicion because they could not show the police officers that they definitely had nothing to do with the new outbreak of vandalism.

'Hey,' said Gilly, 'I wonder whether the two are Pete and Titch.'

'Pete and Titch? Who are they?' inquired Christine.

Gilly explained the patrol set-up of the High

Flyers and the Manton Mobsters, and how she had met the two boys last night.

'You didn't see Caroline Mayhew, by any chance?' asked Christine.

'Yes, I did. Why?'

'Because Caroline saw you with the boys. Her father is now ringing up other parents and committee members to say that you must know something about this latest damage.'

'This is monstrous!' cried Mrs Denham indignantly. 'I'll give him damage, indeed!' She reached for the telephone.

'No, wait!' said Mr Denham quickly. 'Gilly, I must ask you this – did you have anything to do with last night's vandalism?'

'Of course I didn't!' cried Gilly, feeling tears coming to her eyes.

'That's good enough for me,' said her father angrily. 'Now if the club are going to take the attitude that Gilly has done wrong, then she is giving up her membership right now!'

'Mr Denham, as far as John Hanley and I are concerned, Gilly is innocent. There is no proof whatsoever of her involvement and thus no reason for her to leave the club. John is having a word with Mr Mayhew this evening when he returns from a regional meeting and you may be assured that there will be no more telephone calls. There may even be an apology.'

'The situation at the club will still be a hard one for Gilly to take,' said Mrs Denham.

'Yes, you're right,' agreed Christine. 'Some stupid people will want to believe the worst.'

The three grown-ups looked at Gilly.

'Gilly,' said Christine, 'while John and I and most of the people in the club refuse to believe that you are connected with last night's incident, there are some gymnasts and their parents who are convinced that you are. Before long these people will realize that you are completely innocent, but in the meantime they could make you feel pretty uncomfortable.'

'What do you mean?' asked Gilly.

Her mother broke in. 'She means that on training nights, some gymnasts could be really unfriendly. They could say unpleasant things to you or ignore you entirely. They could also hide your kit and generally try to make life miserable for you. So you've got to make a decision.'

'A decision?' Gilly was bewildered.

'Yes, darling,' said her father. 'You must make up your mind whether to stay away from the club until the situation has blown over or to continue training regardless of what other members may say or do to you. We'll back you whatever you decide.'

'There's nothing to decide,' said Gilly determinedly. 'I'm not gong to stop training just because some crazy people could have it in for me.'

'Good girl, Gilly Denham!' said Mr Denham proudly. 'You'll show them yet, eh?'

'John and I will make sure that matters do not get out of hand, certainly during training,' said

82

Christine, 'but you must tell us if someone becomes particularly objectionable.'

'All right,' replied Gilly, knowing that she would never tell tales about anyone.

'Now I'd like to hear more about the boys at Manton Street,' said Christine. 'They seem to be better friends of the club than most people realize.'

'They certainly are,' agreed Gilly, 'and they're far from being vandals.'

She then described how the five boys had played in the old factory and how they had resented the buying of the building by the gym club because they now had nowhere in the neighbourhood where they could meet for games. She also explained how the boys had been helping to keep an eye on the building with the aim of becoming members of the new boys' section of the club when it was formed.

'That's an excellent idea, Gilly!' said Christine. 'We must talk further with John about it. But for the moment, we must hope that the present turmoil at the club dies down soon.'

At school on Monday, Marcia was furious.' 'It's bad enough dealing with vandals but when you've got people on your own side stirring up trouble, it's just plain crazy! If anyone dares to say or do anything to you at training, I'll show them a thing or two!'

Before Gilly left for the gym club the next evening, her mother took her aside.

'Gilly, the best club in the world is not worth attending if you're going to have a miserable time. So don't feel you have to stay there out of duty.'

'Don't worry, Mum!' said Gilly, hugging her. 'I'll be okay, just you see.'

Her mother was right. There was definitely an unfriendly atmosphere at the church hall, with many of the other novices scowling at her while whispering among themselves. The High Flyers stayed close to her, on the lookout for trouble.

Just before the warm-up, a voice called out 'Vandal!' and several gymnasts laughed.

Marcia moved forward angrily, her eyes searching rapidly for the owner of the voice.

Gilly held her back by the arm. 'Marcia, never mind! I can put up with it.'

For the rest of the evening, most of the other novices, Caroline Mayhew among them, ignored her. But several times, Gilly was shoved in the back or tripped. She tried hard to show that she did not mind, but after one hard knock which sent her sprawling, she found it very hard not to cry. She got up to find Marcia confronting Caroline.

'If you do that again – ' growled Marcia.

John Hanley strode quickly over to them. 'This is not a school for wrestlers, it's a gymnastics club!' he said sternly. 'Anyone behaving like a hooligan can go straight home!'

After that, Gilly was left alone. But at the end of the evening, she could not find her kit bag. After a long search by the High Flyers, it was found by Stephanie hidden behind the old upright piano that stood by the stage.

'This is going too far,' said Stephanie to her friends, 'but what can we do?'

At home, Gilly let her tears flow – tears she had controlled successfully during the evening. Mrs Denham tried to comfort her. 'Stay away from the club for a week or two – I'm sure everything will have sorted itself out by then.'

Gilly shook her head. 'I'm not going to give in. I'll find some way out of this mess.' She blew her nose, kissed her mother and went to bed.

With thoughts whirling around her mind, she found it hard to get to sleep. Next morning, her mother had to wake her and she was nearly late for school. But she had a plan of action and during the break she cornered Marcia and Hazel.

'I've decided that I can't just do nothing and let people believe that I have helped the vandals. I've got to find out who those terrible yobbos are.'

'Any ideas?' asked Marcia. 'What can you do that the police and watchdog committee, not to mention the High Flyers and the Manton Mobsters, have not done already?'

'I'm going to see Harry this evening and find out if he noticed anything odd last weekend, anything at all.'

Marcia and Hazel thought that there was little that Harry could add to what was already known. However, it was certainly worth trying him out. As Marcia had to go to the dentist, Hazel offered to come to Manton Street with her.

The girls found the old watchman in a cheerful mood. As ever, he produced two steaming mugs of tea.

'How's your clubhouse?' he asked, pointing with his thumb at the old factory.

'Nearly finished, Harry,' said Gilly, sipping her tea slowly. 'But it got painted again by idiots last weekend as you know.'

'Yep, I does know. Didn't see nobody strange then, I didn't. That's what I tell the police.'

'Did you see anybody at all late in the evening?' asked Gilly.

'Well, I see your usual lot early, all going home – those two lads as well. Then I take a stroll with my flashlight and see your coaches – they was packing up about ten o'clock. The lads came back a little later to check the street. I know they ain't done nothing. And that's all I see.'

Gilly's interest was aroused. 'What coaches, Harry?'

'Two blokes they was. In yeller suits like all your crowd wear. They was putting something in a bag. Tools, I suppose – couldn't see exactly what.'

'Did you see them leave Manton Street?' asked Hazel.

'No, no. Before I came back here, I look in at the pub for a quick beer. They probably went then.'

'Did they have a car?' asked Gilly.

'Car? Don't know. Didn't hear no car.'

I wonder who they were, thought Gilly. I was at the old factory during the afternoon and I can't remember any men coaches in yellow tracksuits.

The two girls thanked Harry and went off together.

'There's something that isn't right about those

coaches,' said Gilly. 'I think it's worth finding out more.'

The girls parted in the town centre and Gilly went home to start her homework as she had to write a report on the world's rice industry by Friday.

Later that evening, she telephoned Mr Galloway. He had worked all out to get the ugly words of red paint removed from the factory wall by the beginning of the week, and was still feeling very tired.

'What can I do for you, Gilly?' he asked with a friendly voice. He knew that Gilly would never be involved in any form of vandalism, particularly as she had carried out so much work at the new headquarters.

Gilly explained that she had heard that two men coaches had worked late at Manton Street on Saturday and that she would like to talk to them. Could Mr Galloway tell her who they were?

Mr Galloway, thinking Gilly needed someone to witness that she had nothing to do with the paint smearing, was puzzled. 'I'm sorry, Gilly, but it's not true that anyone stayed late at the factory. I was the last to leave, and I left at eight o'clock.'

Gilly thanked him and assembled her thoughts again. If the men seen by Harry weren't gym club coaches, who were they? Where did they get the yellow tracksuits? How did they arrive at the factory without being seen by Harry? Then suddenly she remembered. Two tracksuits had been stolen when the vandals had broken into the building some weeks ago. There could well be a link with the two men seen on Saturday.

Gilly telephoned the Narrow Boat and asked Mr O'Connor for Sean. He took a long time to come to the phone and when he did he sounded tired and low-spirited.

'What's the matter?' asked Gilly.

'Look, the Manton Mobsters want to stop patrolling for your club. All we are getting out of it is more and more attention from the fuzz. And as you know, nothing has happened to make it at all worthwhile for us.'

'Sean, you can't pack it in now. Something has happened.' Gilly outlined the latest developments, hoping Sean would change his mind.

After some thought, Sean agreed that there could be a connection between the so-called coaches and the vandalism, but how could they prove there was. What did Gilly suggest as the next step?

'We must search further around the neighbourhood and not just concentrate on Manton Street,' said Gilly, her mind made up. 'With a bit of luck, we might find people who have seen these ugly customers.'

Sean was doubtful that Gilly's new plan would produce any new clues at all. However, he decided to try the idea out for one last time, if it would help free the boys from the suspicion hanging over them. He told Gilly reluctantly that he would ask the Mobsters to tour all around the neighbourhood. 'But whether they will now is a different matter,' he said as he hung up.

Fingers crossed, thought Gilly. Mobsters, we need you – badly.

By Saturday, Christine's guess that Mr Mayhew would apologize for suggesting that Gilly had a part in damaging the factory proved correct. He wrote a short letter to the Denhams saying that he was sorry for being mistaken, and sent copies to the parents and committee members whom he had approached during the previous weekend. As a result, the Denhams decided to try and forget the matter as best they could.

At the morning training session, several gymnasts came up to Gilly to say how sorry they were, too, for thinking she was linked in some way with the defacing of the wall. With a smile, she told them not to worry about it. Despite these gestures of friendship, however, she found her reputation in the club had taken a hard knock and that Caroline Mayhew and her followers had not changed their hostile attitude towards her one bit.

'Hop it, weed!' ordered Marcia as one of the Mayhew gang tried to barge into Gilly as part of her vault.

Gilly knew that she would have to make great efforts to regain even some of her popularity and she was more determined than ever to find out who was behind the campaign to drive Lincston Gymnastics Club out of Manton Street.

Before training, Christine told the novices that their floor and vault competition was definitely going to be held. It was going to be held to show that those girls who had passed Award 1 could perform confidently when they had to compete against other gymnasts. In her heart, Gilly knew that the competition was another way of testing the novices for the elite squad.

The testing session for Award 1 was coming up soon and all ten movements had to be passed to satisfy John and Christine. Gilly could already perform nine of the ten – but a good back flip was still defeating her.

She wrote in her diary about the back flip: '*From the standing position, bend your knees and lean back. Then shoot your arms upward while forcing your body into the air, keeping your legs stretched and hips high in flight. Bring your arms to the floor and move through the handstand position. Push off with your hands from the floor and bring your legs down together to stand.*'

For a long time, Gilly could not trust herself to lean back, even with a coach standing near to support her. But she could now perform a back flip of sorts and she was determined to improve it for the test. However, next day she heard news that made her forget all about it.

Sean rang up excitedly: 'Gilly, Pete's found something which a little old lady has hung on her clothesline! Guess what – it's a yellow tracksuit top!'

Chapter 8

Gilly did a hop, skip and a jump of joy. 'Whoopee!' she called to no one in particular, 'now we're getting somewhere! Good old Mobsters!'

Her father looked over the bannister above her. 'Learned a new move, have you?'

'Not exactly learned a new move, Dad, it's one that's happened!'

She went back to the phone. 'Sean, we better go and see this – did you say little old lady?'

'Yes,' said Sean, 'a little old lady. Come down to the pub after school tomorrow and we'll go on from there.'

Gilly wondered what a little old lady was doing with a yellow tracksuit top. Surely it must be one of the missing club ones. They would find out tomorrow for sure.

At school the next day, she found Marcia and Hazel discussing Olympic gymnastics champions.

'Who is your favourite all-round champion, Gilly?' asked Marcia. 'Mine is Elena Davidova of Russia who won in 1980. She's such a nice person as well as being a good gymnast.'

'Well,' said Hazel, 'I like Mary Lou Retton, the 1984 American winner. She has bags of personality and plenty of attack.'

Gilly said unhesitatingly: 'I go for Nadia Comaneci of Romania. Her victory in 1976 was amazing – seven perfect tens she scored. But it's a shame she rarely smiled.'

'If you think about it,' said Marcia, 'you can't compare champions because the sport is changing the whole time.'

'True,' agreed Gilly, 'every year the moves seem to get harder and more exciting. By the way, I've got some great news.' She told her friends about Pete's find and said that Sean and she were going to investigate that afternoon. Anyone coming?

Hazel had a piano lesson but Marcia was free. 'Fantastic – it's the best bit of luck we've had. Blast, look at the time – I've got to get to chemistry. See you later!'

After school, Gilly and Marcia cycled down to the Narrow Boat where Sean and Pete were waiting for them on their bikes. To the surprise of the girls, the boys took them back up the hill for a short distance and then along a road to the left.

'Where on earth are we going?' asked Gilly.

'We've got to cross the canal,' answered Sean. 'Look, we turn down here.'

They had reached a road which led down the hill again to a narrow hump-backed bridge spanning the canal.

'Watch out for lorries,' said Sean. 'There's not much room for traffic to pass.'

On the other side of the bridge, Sean got off his bike and carried it down some steps to the towpath on the left. The others did the same. Then Sean led them along the towpath, a narrow track which ran alongside the murky water of the canal.

'Look,' said Gilly to Marcia, 'we're opposite the factory.'

She was right. They looked across the canal to the familiar old building and the low wall between it and the water. It was a view that the girls had never seen before and one which, with all the other former warehouses along the canal, made them feel that they were in a town of an earlier age. As in Manton Street, many of the buildings were derelict and due for demolition. It was a deserted and decaying neighbourhood.

'Where to, now?' asked Gilly, not wanting to stay there longer than she had to.

'It's not far,' said Pete, overtaking Sean.

Before long, the warehouses gave way to a mixture of small buildings – sheds, garages and terraced cottages. Then they came to a stretch of the towpath which had been concreted so that boats could tie up there on mooring rings. Opposite this hard-standing and between two red-brick cottages was an opening for vehicles to drive down to the canal. The cottages had small gardens with low fences between them and the towpath and Pete stopped at the one on the right.

'Here we are,' he said as he leaned his bike against the fence. Gilly noticed that there was a clothes-line in the garden but with no tracksuit top hanging on it. The gang entered the garden by a gate and Gilly knocked on the back door.

'Who is it?' called a quavery voice.

'I've come about the tracksuit,' said Gilly loudly.

The door opened and a little woman looked out. She's like my granny, thought Gilly, but a lot shorter and with whiter hair.

'Tracksuit? Oh, I know what you mean. Just wait here, dear.'

The old lady returned, with a big pink shawl around her shoulders and carrying, to Gilly's joy, a neatly-folded tracksuit top of the Lincston Gymnastics Club.

'Did you lose it, dear? It looks a bit big for you.'

'A friend at our club sort of lost it,' said Gilly,

'and we heard that you found it.' She looked around at Marcia and the boys.

'It was lucky, you know,' said the old lady. 'I just happened to go into the garden to call for Marmaduke – he's my cat – when your friend drove off in his van. It was really quite dark but I could see this jacket lying there as it's yellow. When I brought it inside, I noticed it was ever so dirty and so I washed it. But these red paint marks – I couldn't do much about them.'

Gilly's eyes darted to the tracksuit top. Red paint marks – they must have something to do with the painted letters on the factory wall, she thought excitedly.

'Excuse me,' said Marcia, 'but how did you know that this jacket belonged to the man in the van?'

'Well,' replied the old lady, 'I've seen him and his friend here once or twice before and they both have these jackets. They put them on when they arrive.'

'I suppose they were here about half past nine last Saturday night,' said Gilly, remembering that the men were seen at Manton Street at about ten o'clock.'

'Half past nine? No, earlier than that, I'd say. It's still a strange time to go boating, but you'll know more about that than I do.'

'Boating?' Gilly, Marcia and Sean spoke together in surprise.

'Yes, boating. They take this boat off the rack on the top of the van, put it in the water, jump in, and away they go.' The old lady gave the tracksuit top to Gilly and made a scything motion with her arms.

'This time, they came back in an hour or so and hurried away.'

Bert piped up. 'Looks as if they were in a canoe.'

Gilly turned to the old lady. 'Is their boat long and narrow like a big cigar, with two big holes to sit in?'

'That's right, it is. Very unsteady it looks, too.'

'And what colour is it?' asked Sean.

'Oh I don't know, dear – some dark colour. You can't tell properly at night. Maybe blue or green.'

'Can you tell us anything about the van?' asked Gilly.

The old lady began to get agitated. 'I don't think you should be asking me all these questions if those men are friends of yours. Give that jacket back to me.'

Gilly tried to soothe her. 'Please, Mrs – '

'Macdonald,' said the old lady. 'Now I don't want any part in – '

'Mrs Macdonald, we need your help,' said Gilly. 'This tracksuit top was stolen from our club and we are trying to find out who stole it. That's why it's important we know all you can remember.'

The old lady looked at the four in turn, deciding whether to trust them. 'Well,' she said finally, 'there's nothing much I can say about the van. It's old, square-looking, quite large, like a Post Office van – '

'But not red,' interrupted Marcia.

'Oh no, not red. Again, it could be dark blue.'

'Can you remember anything special about it,'

96

asked Sean. 'You know, the licence number, any sign on the sides, any marks, anything.'

'No, it's just a plain van. Ah, I do remember something, if it's helpful. One of the windows is smashed, the one on the right-hand door at the back. Now I really do think that's all I can tell you. That jacket – you'd better take it away.' She turned to go inside her cottage.

'Mrs Macdonald, thank you indeed,' said Gilly. 'We won't bother you again.' Unless we have to, she thought.

The four rode back to Manton Street, delighted with their fresh clues. Gilly stuffed the tracksuit top inside her own jacket so that she looked fatter than usual. 'I'll keep this for the time being,' she said. 'It's a vital clue.'

'What do we do next?' asked Bert, pleased that his discovery had given them a lead at last.

'We better have a meeting with all the Flyers and Mobsters,' said Gilly. 'We can make plans then. But we must get a move on.'

To her disappointment, the first day possible for a meeting was the following Wednesday. Events at home, school and club prevented both boys and girls from being free until then.

'Okay,' said Sean, 'Wednesday it is. We can meet in the pub. Before opening,' he added hastily.

Gilly said: 'Let's not tell anyone about today until the meeting. It's just possible that the crooks could find out how much we know about them and they could decide on different ways of attacking the club.'

At home that evening, Mr Denham peered at his daughter over the top of his newspaper.

'Penny for your thoughts, Gilly,' he said kindly. 'You've obviously got something on your mind.'

'Oh, I've been thinking about some work I've got to do,' said Gilly vaguely.

She had been piecing together all the facts that she had learned that afternoon and before, and the result went something like this.

The vandals were two men who wore stolen Lynx tracksuits to make people think that they, the men, belonged to the gym club. They had never been seen in Manton Street because they came to the old factory by canoe in the dark, climbing over the low wall by the carpark. They had never been heard coming or going because a canoe makes no noise. They probably brought the paint and tools they needed in the canoe. When they had finished their damage, they paddled back to the van which was parked further up the canal and drove off.

Gilly could now prove to the club and to the police that neither she nor the Mobsters had anything to do with the defacing of the factory. But before she did that, there were still two questions to which she had to find the answers: Who were the vandals? Where was their base? However, nothing more could be done until the meeting on Wednesday.

In the meantime, she, Marcia and Melanie had an interesting club outing on Saturday. The Lynx senior team travelled to compete against Fellingham Gymnastics Club in a round of the national club knockout competition. The three girls went along with other club members and their parents as spectators.

In the morning, the team of six girls and a reserve, their leader John Hanley and the spectators met at the church hall to board the coach which the club had hired. It was a three-hour drive to the Fellingham Sports Centre and Gilly and her friends munched sandwiches as they watched the countryside go by.

The sports centre was big, new and full of facilities such as a swimming pool, indoor bowling green and squash courts.

'Wow, what a smashing place!' exclaimed Gilly as they took their seats in one of the centre's several gymnasiums where the four pieces of apparatus – vault, asymmetric bars, beam and floor – were installed.

'It's not quite as good as it looks,' said Marcia. 'Like us at the church hall, the gymnasts can't leave their equipment up. And they haven't got a training pit like we are going to have at Manton Street.'

To the beat of stirring music – played on tape – the competing gymnasts marched on in line to be presented to the crowd before the match started.

'Those leotards are a bit dull,' said Gilly, looking at the dark blue colour worn by the Fellingham team.

'Tell you something for free. That kind of blue is no good for photographs, either,' said Marcia, clapping her hands in time with the march.

The competition was the first that Gilly had watched. Each piece of apparatus was judged by four judges whose scores were taken to their head judge by young Fellingham gymnasts acting as messengers. The head judge, who made sure the judging was fair, crossed out the top and bottom scores and averaged the middle two for a final score. The highest score possible was 10.00 – a perfect score.

Marcia explained: 'If you have four scores of 8.6, 8.7, 8.4 and 8.3, you take out the 8.7 and 8.3 and average the 8.6 and the 8.4. So what's the final score?'

'I get it,' said Gilly, '8.5 – but what happens to the score then?'

'It goes first to the competition's chief scorer and then on to the scoreboard by the apparatus for display.'

Gilly learned that to keep track of the match, spectators had to watch the scoreboard, write the scores in their programmes and add them up. It was the only way the spectators could tell who was winning, for no announcement about the leading gymnast would be made until the end of the match.

At Fellingham, the gymnasts performed voluntary exercises, which Gilly knew were made up by each girl and her coach according to the rules of the world governing body of the sport. For both teams, the lowest score on each piece by a team member did not count when all the scores were added up.

The competition was controlled from a desk by an announcer who introduced each gymnast and gave out scores through loudspeakers. Beside him sat the official who played the tapes of the floor exercise music and the marches to which the gymnasts moved from apparatus to apparatus.

From the start of the match, the Fellingham girls proceeded to trounce their Lincston rivals. Despite an excellent performance by Anita Douglas, the Lynx team finished several marks behind.

'If only Lynn Hobday and Veronica Tatlow were with us still,' said Marcia bitterly.

It was plain to see, though, that the Lynx gymnasts made plenty of mistakes. Except for Anita, all fell off the beam. Two girls stepped outside the floor area and there were some unsteady landings during the vaulting. As Gilly realized, mistakes such as these cost marks.

But more important than the mistakes, there was a feeling that the Lincston gymnasts had not tried their best. The trip home in the coach that evening was a gloomy one, and Gilly wondered whether the recent vandalism and the events connected with it at the club were in some way responsible for the low spirits of their gymnasts. Certainly, John as chief coach had more than enough problems.

By the following Tuesday, Gilly had a big problem of her own. She had completely forgotten that she was due to take Award 1 soon, and so was taken by surprise when Christine announced that each novice would be tested for the award starting that evening.

Gilly had been so concerned with the happenings at Manton Street that she had not bothered to improve her back flip or polish up the other nine movements. As a result, her test was a shambles which brought her closer to tears than all the animosity of Caroline Mayhew and her friends.

John said bluntly afterwards: 'Gilly, I know you've

had a bad time lately, but you clearly haven't bothered to cope with what was a simple test of concentration. You knew that the coming novice competition was important if you wanted to take the sport seriously. After that fiasco, we can't possibly let you enter the competition and, what's more, your attitude could get you chucked out of the club!'

Chapter 9

The High Flyers and the Manton Mobsters sat in the salon bar of the Narrow Boat in shy silence. Nothing could be heard except for the munching of the crisps which Mrs O'Connor had provided for the Tuesday afternoon meeting.

Gilly tried hard to fight against the gloomy feeling

she had had ever since the night before when she failed her Award 1 test at the gym club. Nothing ever seems to go right for me, she thought. People now think that I'm a failure as well as being someone who gets into trouble easily.

Glancing up, she noticed everyone looking at her. She realized that it was up to her to organize the next step of tracking down the vandals of the club's new headquarters. With an effort, she pulled herself together and faced her friends.

'We're here because, thanks to Pete, we've found out a lot about the horrible people who have been ruining the old factory.'

Pete turned red and nearly choked on a crisp.

Gilly explained for the benefit of the Flyers and the Mobsters who had not heard the latest developments how Pete had found the tracksuit top which in turn had led them to discovering from Mrs Macdonald about the two main suspects – the men with a van.

She continued: 'But we still don't know who the men are and we've got to carry on trying to track them down. They haven't caused any damage to the building for some time and I bet they're planning another raid right now.'

'But how do they get to Manton Street after they've parked the van some distance away?' asked Melanie.

'By canoe,' said Gilly.

'What – by *canoe*?' Titch could not believe what he had heard. His fellow Mobsters looked at each other in surprise.

'Yes, by canoe.' Gilly told them how the men used their canoe to approach the factory silently and without being seen.

'I can't believe it,' said Rob, shaking his head in amazement. 'No wonder they haven't been rumbled and no wonder we never spotted them.'

'Oh my,' said Shani, 'then they are driving away in their van.'

'Yes,' said Sean, the scowl leaving his face, 'and that's the next part of the trail.'

'What do you mean?' asked Stephanie.

'The van – we've got to find that van,' said Gilly determinedly, 'and once we've done that we'll know how to get the crooks.'

'Surely it's a job for the fuzz,' said Lofty. 'How can we possibly find the van? It could be miles away.'

'It's got to be somewhere in Lincston,' said Gilly. 'Surely only local baddies would bother with messing up the gym club. I have a feeling the police won't want to spend time looking for a van that some kids think is linked with the Manton Street goings-on.'

'So we would go to the police when we've found something?' asked Marcia.

'Yes – or if we don't find anything,' said Gilly.

There was a further period of silence while everyone thought the matter over.

Then Hazel spoke up. 'How do we go about finding something which could be in a million trillion places – even in a place as small as Lincston?'

Gilly reached into her satchel and pulled out what looked like a folder. 'Here's a map of the town –

it's my dad's. I think we should all look in different places, near to where we live.' She spread the map out on a table and the others crowded around. 'I've marked where all us Flyers live. And here's Manton Street.'

The map showed, as everyone knew, that the girls lived away from the centre of Lincston while the homes of the boys were all in the Manton Street area.

'It's going to take a fair bit of time to cover the whole town,' said Sean, studying the map closely. 'We'll have to work something out so that once one neighbourhood's been searched, we can go on to another straight away.'

'Anyone disagree?' asked Gilly. 'No – well, that's exactly what we'll do. Now let's start with the north side of the canal . . .'

By the time their meeting ended, each girl and boy knew exactly which district they were responsible for. The boys had the job of covering the more crowded business centre of Lincston while the girls were to look all over the residential areas.

'We've got to explore just everywhere,' Gilly told them, 'down side streets, behind buildings, over fences – anywhere where a van could be parked or hidden. Remember, it's a dark van, maybe blue or green, with a rack on top with perhaps a canoe fixed to it, and it has a smashed back window on the right. The canoe will be a dark colour, too.'

'If you find the van,' said Sean, 'don't stay around. Tell me or Gilly right away. Those guys are dangerous, as we know.'

That was the beginning of what became known as the Great Search. It meant long hours of biking the streets and roads of Lincston in all weathers. It was tiring, boring and difficult at times. On many occasions, the young searchers were chased out of private roads and courtyards where they were trespassers.

Once Gilly was frightened badly when she was standing on her bike, trying to look through the high windows of a garage on the Weston Park Estate. A hand descended heavily on her shoulder.

'What's up, kiddo?' said a deep, gruff voice. It was a man with a thick black beard and green overalls. 'Or do I have to get the police?'

'I'm sorry,' said Gilly, trying not to tremble. 'I was just looking for something.'

'And what might that be?' asked Blackbeard.

'A dark van with a canoe on top.'

'There's nothing like that around here. So hop it if you don't want to get into trouble.

Gilly rode away in relief. There were many garages in the part of Lincston which was her territory and they all had to be checked, even if it meant a return visit. Naturally, she did not want the people who used the garages to think that she was up to no good.

After a few days, the High Flyers and the Mobsters met again to discuss progress. So far, there was no news to act on and Gilly could feel that one or two of the searchers were losing their interest in the search. As each boy and girl reported on the areas already visited, Gilly marked the map with pencil so they could see which places remained unexplored. While she was doing this, she noticed that Shani had not covered much ground.

'Shani, you've hardly started,' she said, looking at the map.

Shani grimaced. 'My parents are not liking me to go around the streets by myself. So I am doing a little at a time.'

'We may have to help you out,' said Gilly, 'but we can't at the moment.'

'It's time we're short of,' said Sean. 'I bet we could search the whole town in a couple of days if we didn't have to go to school.'

Marcia agreed. 'Of course we could. At the same time, we could go on looking for ever if nothing turns up.' She glanced at Gilly.

'Let's give it another week,' said Gilly. 'If we haven't had more luck by then – well, we'll go to the police.'

Later, when she and Marcia were sitting in the Moo-Moo Milk Bar, she said she was pleased at how keen their group was to hunt the van down.

'I know what you mean,' said Marcia. 'That's why I'm sure we're going to be lucky before long.'

'Well, I don't mind telling you that I'm worried about Shani – she's done so little so far.'

'Shani? She's the last person to worry about. She'll find a way to finish her part of the search.'

I've got lots of worries, thought Gilly – the vandals, Shani, the gym club, to mention a few. And my biggest worry is the gym club.

Ever since she failed her Award 1 and therefore

her entry to the novice competition, Gilly's popularity with both her fellow gymnasts and her coaches had suffered a further knock. Of the best girls in the novice squad, Gilly and two others – Toni Williamson and Geraldine Jones – were the only ones not to pass this important stage. There was some excuse for Toni and Geraldine because Toni had an ankle sprain at the time and Geraldine was away with a heavy cold, but most people felt that Gilly should have come through the test with ease.

Another worry for Gilly was that she was in danger of being separated from her friends in the High Flyers who had all passed Award 1. If they went into the elite squad without her, they would train at different times from the novice squad and so she would not meet them as often as she did now.

Gilly knew that the only way to regain her popularity at the club was to work hard. Within the novice squad, she tried not to do anything to provoke more jealousy and dislike. She stayed as quiet and modest as she could and made sure that she praised outstanding moves performed by other girls. She also made a point of looking out for situations where she could be helpful to other gymnasts during training. For example, she became quick to notice when anyone needed support when practising a move such as a handstand, or wanted bracing when performing a suppling exercise.

To win back the full approval of her coaches, Gilly knew that she must get her back flip right as well as showing that she had mastered all the movements she had been taught. She realized that John and Christine had backed her against anyone in the club who thought she was linked with the damage at the new headquarters, but she was aware that in the end her future at the club depended on her own progress in the sport. Her goal now was to persuade the two coaches to allow her to retake the test she had failed. For if she could not pass Award 1, she could give up all hope of joining the elite squad.

I must get into the elite squad, thought Gilly, I must, I must. Once I'm there, things will begin to get really exciting – like more work on the asymmetric bars and beam, like more important competitions. I've got to do it somehow . . .

Then time began to run out. At the next Tuesday training session, John announced that the novice competition would take place in ten days time on a Saturday, followed a week later by the official opening of the new Manton Street headquarters.

Gilly began to panic. I will have to get a move on, she thought, or I'll miss my chance. Recently, she had achieved another important movement – the handspring vault. The handspring vault was a vital skill to learn and Christine made her novices practise it again and again. Gilly learned how to keep her body straight as she took off from the springboard, thrusting with her hands from the horse as her body rotated for the landing.

'Not bad, young lady, not bad,' said John approvingly as Gilly made a perfect landing while he stood

110

near the horse to 'spot' or support any vaulter who needed help.

Gilly blushed with pride. Now if she could only get the hang of the back flip . . .

That evening, she knew it was now or never – success or failure. Once she could perform the back flip reasonably well, John and Christine could hardly stop her taking Award 1 again. What's more, they must have seen that she had worked pretty hard at the last few training sessions.

As if understanding her thoughts, Christine came up to her. 'Okay, Gilly, let's see your back flip.'

They moved on to a floor mat. Christine watched while Gilly stood still, trying to concentrate. Oh, what the heck, she thought and flung herself backwards and upwards. To her amazement, she succeeded, ending with her feet secure on the floor and her arms outstretched above her.

'Good girl!' said Christine. 'Do it again.' Which Gilly did. By the time she went home, she felt she had done the back handspring all her life. She was so overjoyed that she completely forgot to ask Christine whether she could take the test again. When she got home, she consulted her mother about what she should do next.

'Give Christine or John a ring tomorrow,' advised Mrs Denham. 'I'm sure they'll let you have another go. Talking of telephoning, Shani rang a few minutes ago. She said it was important.'

Gilly swallowed her soup and reached for the telephone. What did Shani want at this time of night? Why didn't she say anything at the club?

Shani took some time to get to the point. 'I thought it would be better telling you after gym and not during it when you are working so much. Also, as you said, it's best to keep important things secret so the wicked people are not finding out.'

'So what's news?' asked Gilly, her curiosity growing.

'Gilly, I am thinking I have found the van!'

Chapter 10

Gilly spent a long time that evening talking on the telephone.

'I was absolutely thrilled,' she said happily when she told Marcia later that evening about Shani's discovery. 'But I had to find out exactly where the van was before I got really excited.'

'You think you're excited,' cried her friend. 'Well, I'm just over the moon. Clever old Shani – I just knew she would pull something off. But where is the van?'

Gilly explained how Shani that afternoon had ambled with her little sister Muni through a small and untidy industrial estate just off Watkins Street in her search area. The estate had several businesses on it – businesses such as a scrap metal merchant, timber contractor and coal depot. Each company had an office or warehouse building on the estate road with a yard behind it for storing supplies. Shani had slipped quickly into each yard to spy out for the van. She struck lucky at the end of the estate road.

'There's a builder's warehouse there,' said Gilly, 'with a yard full of junk and a wooden shed in the far corner which is used for an office. There was no one around so Shani had a look around the yard. She was just about to leave when she spotted – guess what – a dark green canoe beside the shed.'

'Crumbs!' exclaimed Marcia. 'A canoe – but no van?'

'No van. But Shani reckoned that before long someone would return to the yard and then she could see for certain whether a dark van was based there.'

'But she didn't stay in the yard.'

'Heavens no! She and Muni played with a ball in the estate road, waiting for something to happen. She was scared stiff.'

After an hour, Muni became tired and bored, wanting to go home. Shani reluctantly agreed and they set off towards Watkins Street. At that moment, a lorry drove down the road and entered the builder's yard. Shani hesitated, and then took the protesting Muni and skipped along towards the warehouse, her heart beating. They were overtaken by an old navy blue van which also drove into the yard. Shani knew immediately that her search had ended.

'Why?' asked Marcia.

'Because the window was smashed on the back right-hand door.'

'I'm jiggered,' said Marcia. 'That girl deserves a medal. What happened next?'

'Well, the van parked beside the shed and the two drivers came around to the front, talking to each other. Apparently they were rough-looking characters – and sounded that way, too. Then a third man in a posh car drove up and seemed to give them orders. Shani decided that enough was enough, so she and Muni scarpered. Anyway, she had gym club to get to and she didn't want to be late.'

'So what do we do now?' Marcia's voice had a quaver in it.

'You and I, Miss Cherry, go and look at that yard for ourselves – on Saturday. I've asked Shani not to say anything until our meeting afterwards.'

Marcia was silent for a moment. Then she said brightly: 'All right, Miss Denham, Saturday afternoon it is.'

As soon as Gilly put the phone down, it rang.

'Someone's had a long call, young lady,' said a

familiar and cheerful voice. It was John Hanley. 'I've been trying to get you all evening.'

'Sorry about that,' said Gilly, praying that she was going to hear some more good news.

'Gilly, both Christine and I feel as you've been trying so hard at the club recently you should have another crack at Award 1.'

Gilly nearly burst into tears with joy and relief.

'So,' John went on, 'we'll test you on Saturday morning – which gives you a little more time to practise your back flip.'

After Gilly had thanked John, she ran into the sitting room to tell her parents.

'I'm so glad, darling,' said Mrs Denham, looking up from her library book. 'I had a strong feeling the club would let you have another go. Just put all you can into it and I'm sure you'll pass.'

'I *must* pass, Mum,' said Gilly, thinking of her back flip and wishing she had learned it sooner.

'Don't worry, you will,' said her father confidently. He was watching a football match on television. 'By the way, you and that Cherry girl talked on the phone for a good long time, as indeed you did with what's-her-name – Shani. What's brewing?'

'Brewing? Oh, nothing much,' said Gilly, trying to sound as casual as possible. Her father was not deceived.

'You're up to something, that's for sure. All I can say is, don't get into more trouble or you're finished as a member of the gym club.'

It was Gilly's turn to say 'don't worry'. If she did nothing else, she thought, she was determined to

116

make everything come right. Her friends in the High Flyers and Manton Mobsters had all put so much work into patrolling and searching on behalf of the gym club that somehow there had to be happy ending not just for her but for everyone.

Hopefully, the search for the vandals would finish on Saturday and that would end for good the scary possibility of club property – and people – being attacked at any time. Gilly shivered to think about it, as she had done many times before.

Her mother broke into her thoughts. 'You look pretty tired, so why don't you have an early night. You'll feel a lot better for it.'

However, an early night was impossible. Not only did Gilly have her homework to finish, but also she had her Award 1 exercises to practise. Most of the Award's moves could only be performed properly in a gym, but Gilly found that she could carry out handstands and splits without disturbing too much furniture or her parents' nerves.

'You do feel all right, don't you?' asked her mother anxiously.

'Of course I do, Mum,' said Gilly. 'It's just that I have a lot to do.'

She knew really that she should let her mother know about Shani's discovery, but the thought of spending several hours the next day perhaps talking to the police and other people instead of training was more than she could take. There were only three days to go to the test and she did not want to lose one second of time. She gave her mother a kiss and went upstairs to begin her homework.

117

After school the next day, Marcia came up to her. 'Hey, did you tell anyone about Shani?' she asked.

'No,' said Gilly and explained why.

Marcia wrinkled her nose. 'I guessed you wouldn't until we had seen the yard. Anyway, we can go and see the police on Saturday.'

'I won't want to see anyone if I fail Award 1,' said Gilly gloomily.

'Don't be daft,' said her friend firmly. 'You're going to pass and I'm going to see that you do.'

It was exactly like this before my test for the gym club, thought Gilly. Why do I always find life so full of problems?

Marcia took charge of her. 'Come on, we're going to have a bash at all your moves.'

'Where?' asked Gilly.

'Where do you think? In the school gym, of course,' said Marcia, leading her off. 'I've managed to borrow a couple of mats.'

Once again, Marcia became an expert coach. As Gilly began performing each of the ten exercises, she knew that her friend could one day with training become an outstanding teacher of young gymnasts. Pass or fail, she certainly had a lot to thank Marcia for.

Not for the first time Gilly wished that Lincston Gymnastics Club did not insist that their gymnasts had to perform all ten moves perfectly. Normally, only six out of ten needed to be passed to gain the award. So in the empty gym at the High, she progressed through all ten, leaving her weakest exercise, the back flip, until last. Marcia stood by her, keeping a sharp eye on her style. Every now and then, she would give Gilly advice such as 'keep your legs together', or 'head up' or 'back straight'.

Gilly knew the list of moves by heart. It contained the round-off, the handstand through bridge stand, the handspring, forward or sideways splits, the one-hand cartwheel, the kick to handstand, and three movements using the vaulting box. And then there was the back flip, the one exercise which could let her down, the exercise which she had learned only two days before.

Before Gilly tackled the back flip, Marcia sat her down on a bench. 'Look, you've got enough experience to do all those moves blindfolded. I know you can do a smashing back flip as well so just pretend you've done it all your life. Now let's see how well you can do it. Just take your time.'

Gilly stood at the end of the mats and paused for a moment. Then she stood straight, glanced at Marcia – and launched confidently into a neat back flip, landing steadily with her arms above her head in triumph.

Fantastic, she thought thankfully, I can do it, I really can. I haven't forgotten it!

A wide grin spread over Marcia's face. 'Gymnast Gilly, you're on your way. Now do it again.'

By the time the two girls left the school gym, Gilly knew that only an accident could stop her passing the test. But Marcia warned her against relaxing too soon. 'You've got to practise that back flip until the last moment. And that means coming back here tomorrow afternoon.'

By Saturday morning, Gilly felt that she could pass any form of test. Before she cycled off to the club, her mother kissed her goodbye. 'Lots of luck, darling,' she said, brushing some fluff of her daughter's yellow tracksuit. 'Hurry back and tell me all about it.' Mr Denham was at a conference and was not expected back until the late afternoon.

Marcia was coming to the Denhams' for lunch after gym, and then the two girls were going to explore the builder's yard. Afterwards, they were going straight to the Narrow Boat to meet their friends and report on their expedition.

The three girls taking Award 1 – Gilly, Toni Williamson and Geraldine Jones – had been asked to arrive at the Church Hall a little earlier than usual so that they could be tested before training began. Gilly hoped that not many people would be about, but when she arrived she was startled to see that nearly the entire novice squad was present.

Christine came up to her. 'Get warmed up, Gilly, and then we can start straight away. You're first on.'

Gilly, Toni and Geraldine completed their warming-up exercises quickly. Then Gilly took off her tracksuit and waited to begin. Even though she knew she could pass, she still had a fluttery feeling. So much depended on the result.

For the rest of her life, Gilly would remember that morning. She was aware of Caroline Mayhew and her gang, Caroline with a sneer on her face.

She noticed several of the club's coaches taking a great interest. And then she saw her five friends – Marcia, Hazel, Shani, Melanie and Stephanie – standing in a group, urging her silently to succeed. Marcia raised her thumb as if to say again: 'You can do it.'

John Hanley stepped forward with a notebook. 'Okay, Gilly, away you go. Let's see your back flip.'

Everyone stopped talking and turned to watch her. With a big effort, Gilly put everything else out of her mind and concentrated on the test. She went through the ten moves hardly conscious of her audience. When she had completed the last one – the kick to handstand – she heard a murmur of praise from several club members.

Her friends crowded around her with delight. Caroline Mayhew, clearly disappointed at Gilly's performance, gave a loud sniff.

'Smashing,' said Marcia enthusiastically, giving Gilly a bear hug.

'Quiet, please,' called John, 'we haven't finished testing yet.'

While Toni and Geraldine had finished their tests, John and Christine talked together for a few moments. Then John held up his hand for silence.

Here it comes, thought Gilly, crossing her fingers.

However, to her disappointment, John gave out several other announcements to the waiting gymnasts and coaches.

Gilly felt a growing feeling of alarm inside her. We can't have all failed, she wondered, watching the chief coach close his notebook.

John looked up. 'Oh, by the way, I'm delighted to tell you that Geraldine, Toni and Gilly have passed their Award 1.'

Gilly's friends jumped up and down, squealing with joy. Dazed with thankfulness, Gilly went through the rest of the morning's training hardly aware of what was going on. I've done it, I've done it, she told herself, her spirits rising steadily.

Her coaches were delighted, too. After training, Christine said: 'Gilly, I'm very pleased. I've always thought you could become a good gymnast and seeing how you passed today makes me think that even more. Try a little harder – and you could go a long way.'

Mr Cherry also boosted her spirits. 'You're a natural for the elite squad,' he said.

At the end of the morning, Gilly found a moment to whisper 'thanks' to Shani for her important find of the van. Shani was obviously very pleased, and said yes, she was coming to the meeting at the Narrow Boat that afternoon.

Then John came up to Gilly. 'Keep up the good work, that's all we ask.' He then led her aside from her friends. 'By the way, Christine has been telling me about those boys who have been helping the club. What do you know about them?'

Gilly took a deep breath. She described how the five Manton Mobsters had spent long hours patrolling the area looking for signs of the vandals. She was about to tell her chief coach about Pete's discovery of the tracksuit when she realized that she should wait until she had checked the van in the builder's yard before she could tell him the full story. She paused – and wondered why John was asking her about the boys.

John answered her silent question immediately. 'I'd like those lads to join our new boys' squad. They've shown already that they could be a credit to the club.'

Gilly's face showed her pleasure. That's great news, she thought.

'However,' said John, 'I've got to persuade the committee next week that the boys will make good members. Trouble is, several people in the club are still suspicious about the boys – and you, for that matter. They still think you had something to do with the damage to the new headquarters.'

'It's so unfair,' cried Gilly. 'We've worked so hard to stop any more wrecking being done.'

John nodded. 'I know – but the police still have a big black mark against the boys.' He sighed. 'The club really can't get back to normal until the threat of any more vandalism is lifted. I'd like to think that those thugs will now leave us alone, but I have a strong feeling they'll try and cause another upset – just before our official opening next week.'

Not if we can help it, thought Gilly. This afternoon has got to be the last stage of getting those crooks caught, danger or no danger!

Chapter 11

When Gilly and Marcia arrived home for lunch, Mrs Denham could tell from their smiles that Gilly had succeeded in her ordeal. 'I knew you'd do it,' she said delightedly. 'I should have put a bet on you.'

'There's more good news as well, Mum,' said Gilly, and she explained that John was hoping to make the Manton Mobsters members of the gym club.

'I'm very glad to hear that,' said Mrs Denham as she placed a bowl of salad on the table. 'And you girls deserve a bit of praise, too. I'm still not very happy about the way the club has treated you, Gilly. But I can understand that the vandal situation must be cleared up before things at the club get back to rights.'

Gilly and Marcia looked at each other quickly. Gilly cleared her throat. 'That shouldn't take too long. It's time the club had some good luck.'

'You're more hopeful than I am,' said her mother. 'Come on, Marcia, tuck in.'

After lunch, the girls changed out of their leotards and tracksuits.

'Going anywhere special?' asked Mrs Denham.

'Oh, just for a bike ride, Mum.'

The two girls set off, heading for the park.

'We've got plenty of time,' said Gilly, 'and it won't take long to get there.'

They crossed the park and took a short-cut by the hospital to reach Watkins Street. Half a mile along Watkins Street, heading out of Lincston, they came to the estate road.

'Here we are,' said Marcia, 'just like Shani said.' She suddenly pedalled down the estate road as if she did so every day. Gilly caught up with her about half way down it. They coasted to a stop and looked at the end warehouse.

'Blast, the yard's closed,' Marcia pointed out.

There was a tall metal gate which Shani had not mentioned and which was now shut across the entrance which led to the yard behind the warehouse. The gate had unwelcoming barbed wire coiled along its top.

'We've got to get in,' said Gilly, biting her lip.

They stood holding their bicycles. There was no way that the gate would open for them.

'I know,' said Gilly suddenly, 'we'll get on the wall.'

On the other side of the warehouse was a high, rickety-looking wall which ran along the end of several back gardens of some small houses. The wall continued past the warehouse to form a side boundary to the yard.

Marcia frowned. 'How do we climb that? It's far too tall.'

'No problem,' said Gilly. 'We stand on our bikes.'

'Brill!' cried Marcia. The two girls quickly wheeled their bicycles over to the wall, padlocking them together.

Marcia held the bicycles steady while Gilly climbed on to them and grasped the top of the wall.

'Look out for glass,' Marcia called, 'sometimes old walls have jagged pieces stuck in them to put climbers off.'

There was no glass. Gilly pulled herself up on to the top of the wall and sat there while she leaned down to give Marcia a hand. Marcia mounted the wall without difficulty and perched beside her friend. They looked down the road to see if anyone had watched them. There was no one in sight.

'Let's get going,' said Gilly. 'Look, the wall leads straight to the office shed.'

Carefully, the two rose to their feet and walked slowly along the top of the wall, Gilly leading.

This is like when I practised for the beam by walking along a wall, thought Gilly, except this time the wall is much, much higher. She concentrated hard, putting all her effort into keeping her balance. It was a long way down to the ground . . . She wondered if anyone in the houses could see them and whether they would be yelled at.

'Nearly there,' said Marcia as they approached the shed in the corner of the yard. The shed had windows and a door, and stood about half a metre away from the wall. The rest of the yard was filled, as Shani had said, with building materials such as bricks, drainpipes and paving stones. But what interested Gilly most was an old blue van parked on the other side of the shed. The window in its right back door was broken. She nearly fell off the wall with excitement.

'Here we go,' said Gilly. She jumped down on to a pile of planks which reached half way up the wall. Marcia followed, taking care not to dislodge the wood. With a second jump, they were on the ground.

'And there's the canoe.' Gilly pointed to the dark green craft which lay alongside the van. Marcia went up to the van and opened a back door. Inside were two canoe paddles, a tin of petrol, a large box containing a mixture of carpentry tools and iron bars, a can of red paint, and, to prove that the search for the vandals had really come to an end, a yellow Lincston gym club tracksuit thrown on to the floor of the van.

The girls looked at each other in triumph. 'This is it,' said Gilly, her eyes bright with delight. 'Now we really *can* go to the police.'

'The sooner, the better,' agreed Marcia. 'There's no point hanging around here.'

They climbed on to the planks and were just about to remount the wall when they heard a lorry come down the estate road. To their horror, it stopped at the other side of the warehouse.

'Oh no!' cried Marcia, 'it's the lorry which belongs here. It's going to drive in.'

The girls looked around the yard in panic. To get on the wall would mean that they would be spotted immediately. Then Gilly saw their only way of keeping out of sight.

'Quick, down here!' she called in a loud whisper, jumping off the planks.

Marcia followed her and the two girls slipped into the gap between the shed and the wall. They crouched down under a window and listened for any sound which could tell them what was happening. After a minute, they heard the lorry drive in and pull up with a squeal of brakes on the other side of the yard. There were two slams of the driving-cab doors which told the girls that there were two people getting out of the lorry. Then they heard someone unlock the door of the office. After that, two sets of heavy feet clumped across the wooden floor. The girls could hear two men talking but their voices were too faint to hear properly.

Suddenly, without warning, the window above the girls was opened and an empty cigarette packet thrown out which just missed Marcia's head. She gripped Gilly's arm in fright.

Now the voices could be heard clearly. They belonged to two men who appeared to have finished work for the day.

'Come on – let's push off,' said a deep, rasping voice, the one nearest the window. 'You know, the longer I work here, the more I think this shack is like a bleeding third-class horse-box. I'm going to talk to the boss about it when I see him later.'

'Lot of good that will do,' said the other voice which was also loud and tough-sounding. 'He's certainly not going to spend money tarting it up. What's he want you for, anyway?'

'He's talking about a little burn-up this evening. Reckons it's the only way to shift all those flaming wallies he's so uptight about.'

'Well,' said voice number two, 'he's not getting a free service. So tell him that for sure.'

'That's exactly, matey, what I'm going to do. I'll see you later.'

The window was closed again, cutting off the voices. The footsteps clattered away and the door was locked. Gilly and Marcia stayed still and silent until they were certain that the two men had left the yard. Then Gilly peered cautiously around the corner of the shed.

'Let's get out of here,' she whispered with a shiver.

Quietly, the two girls climbed on to the planks

and then on to the top of the wall, looking and listening for any sign that the two men were still around. They then retraced their route along the top of the wall, moving faster than they did before.

'This is more difficult than any beam work,' grumbled Marcia as she wobbled dangerously at one point.

As they approached their bicycles, a woman's voice called out to them from one of the houses. 'You kids, get off the wall!'

The girls were only too glad to. They let themselves down gingerly, with a final jump to clear the wall. Marcia tripped and fell on to her hands with a curse. She had not only stung herself on some nettles but had got mud on her jeans. Glancing around, they unlocked their bicycles and rode off speedily towards Watkins Street.

'Whew, I'm glad that's over,' panted Gilly. 'It couldn't be plainer that those horrible men are the ones we've been looking for.'

'Thank goodness – you won't catch me back there,' declared Marcia, looking over her shoulder in case somebody or something was chasing her. 'By the way, what do you think those stinkos meant by a "burn-up"?'

'I've no idea,' said Gilly. 'Let's get over to the Narrow Boat and tell everyone what we've found out.'

As they coasted along through the streets of Lincston towards Manton Street, Gilly thought again about what the two vandals had said. 'A little burn-up this evening', one of them had mentioned, 'the only way to shift those flaming wallies'. A burn-up sounds like a fire, she thought idly. Fire? She nearly fell off her bicycle as the thought struck her.

'Marcia,' she called out, 'I think something terrible could happen tonight – something terrible to the old factory.'

'What do you mean?' Marcia called back.

'I'm sure those awful men are going to burn it down.'

'Why do you think that, for Pete's sake?' cried Marcia.

'I'll explain when we get to the Narrow Boat.'

By the time they reached the pub, Gilly had remembered something else. In the back of the van in the builder's yard, there had been a tin of petrol – all that was needed to start a fierce blaze.

All five Manton Mobsters were in the closed bar of the Narrow Boat, munching crisps as usual. But, to Gilly's disappointment, she, Marcia and Shani were the only girls present.

'Where are the others?' she asked, beginning to feel desperate. 'We need them here – and how.'

'Probably shopping or something, I should think,' replied Marcia, stealing a crisp from Pete. 'I expect they'll turn up soon.'

'What's up, Gilly?' asked Sean.

As quickly as she could, Gilly told the boys about Shani's discovery and their adventure in the builder's yard. As the boys listened, they became more and more excited, pounding the tables, clapping their hands and calling out.

'Quiet, you lot,' ordered Sean, who was trying

hard not to show how thrilled he was. 'You're like a pack of piglets at the trough.'

He turned to the girls. 'You've done an amazing job, you really have. So now we can hand everything over to the police.'

'It's not as easy as that,' said Marcia. 'Gilly thinks that Manton Street is going to get a fiery visit.'

Everyone looked at Gilly again with puzzled expressions.

'It's only a hunch,' said Gilly, 'but those men talked about a "burn-up to shift those flaming wallies". I think what they meant was that they are planning to burn the club's new headquarters down – yes, burn them down so that we would have to leave Manton Street for ever. And what's more, they talked about "this evening".'

'This evening,' said Sean thoughtfully. He looked up, his scowl returning. 'You could be right. But we don't know for certain.'

'That's what we've got to find out – right now,' said Gilly. 'If they are coming soon, we haven't much time to stop them!'

Chapter 12

Sean leaned across the table. 'And how,' he asked earnestly, 'are *we* going to stop a couple of toughs? It must be a job for the police.'

Gilly said: 'We don't know definitely whether the men are coming to Manton Street or not. So I don't think we can ask the police to come over here and wait for what could be nothing at all.'

Marcia agreed. 'That makes sense,' she told the others.

'However,' Gilly went on, 'if those crooks really are going to try and set fire to our building, what better than if they're caught in the act? Then the police and everyone else would need no more convincing that these men have caused all the trouble.'

'So what can we do?' asked Lofty.

'Well,' said Gilly, her mind beginning to spark off ideas, 'once we know that the two are actually coming to Manton Street, then we would send for the police – through Harry across the road here.'

'That means waiting by the building – and that could be a long time,' Pete pointed out.

'No – we'll arrange a look-out system. We'll need two people for that, and they've got to have bikes.'

Sean gestured to Titch and Rob. 'Better be you two first. We can take turns.'

'So what next?' Titch's voice was full of curiosity.

'There's a phone box in Watkins Street,' said Gilly, 'just past the end of the estate road. Titch, you get over there now and check that the phone's working. Then ring here to tell us what the number of the box is.'

Titch began to get the idea. 'Then I phone if an old blue van with a canoe on top leaves the estate road.'

'You're spot on,' said Gilly. 'Now look – as Pete said, it could be a long time before you see anything. So we'll send someone to relieve you after two hours. Then come back here.'

'So Rob will do the same – from another phone,' said Marcia eagerly.

'That's right,' said Gilly, 'as long as it's close to where the men launch the canoe.'

Sean thought for a moment. 'Can't think of a box around here. Tell you what, lads, we'll pop over and have a look-see. My guess is that if those geezers are coming, they'll wait until it gets dark. That gives us at least three hours.'

Just then Melanie walked in. 'Everyone's looking very serious,' she remarked.

'Good to see you, Mel,' said Marcia. 'We've got a big job on.' She took Melanie aside to explain what was going to happen.

Sean got to his feet. 'Right, Rob, we're off. Titch, you get up to Watkins Street. Lofty, stay by the phone here. We'll have to move into the kitchen once the pub opens. What are you girls going to do?'

'For now, I'm going over to the club head-quarters,' said Marcia. 'The countdown has started for the grand opening and that's only two weeks away.'

'I'll come with you,' said Melanie. 'See you around.'

Gilly and Shani decided to nip back to their homes for a short while. Gilly wanted to try and get Hazel and Stephanie to come down to Manton Street as soon as they could.

Sean looked at his watch. 'Let's all meet here in two hours time. As Gilly says, it could be a long wait.'

Gilly hurried back to her home and surprised her parents who were having a cup of tea. Richard was engrossed with television.

'I thought you were with Marcia,' said Mrs Denham.

'I am, Mum – down at Manton Street. I'm going back there in a couple of hours.'

'What are you up to this time?' asked her father, eating a piece of shortcake.

'Nothing much. I'm going to see if Hazel and Stephanie can join us.'

Gilly seized a piece of shortbread and dashed away to the phone. To her annoyance, Hazel had gone shopping in London that afternoon, while Stephanie was out visiting her godmother. Gilly left messages for the girls to come to Manton Street as soon as they could.

'Life does seem a mad rush for you these days,' said Mr Denham when she returned. 'I sometimes wonder where you get all your energy from. I once thought gymnastics would slow you down. On the contrary, you seem to tear around faster and faster.'

Gilly smiled and took another piece of shortbread.

'Talking of gymnastics,' said her father, 'I'm very pleased indeed that you got through your test today. Tell me about it.'

Gilly settled down to describe how she passed Award 1 that morning. Time passed quickly, and before very long she had to return to the Narrow Boat. She was just about to leave when something told her to take the club tracksuit top which Pete had found at Mrs Macdonald's. Well, it is important evidence, she thought. So she fetched the yellow jacket from the cupboard where it had been since its discovery and put it in a carrier bag.

'When will you get back, darling?' called Mrs Denham from the kitchen.

'Quite late, I expect. 'Bye!'

'Enjoy yourself!' said her father, looking up from his newspaper.

'Thanks, Dad,' said Gilly, wondering if any part of the evening would turn out to be enjoyable.

Richard stuck his tongue out at her as she left through the front door. 'Have fun, gymbo!' he echoed.

Back at the Narrow Boat, Gilly found Sean, Pete and Lofty sitting at the kitchen table while Mr and Mrs O'Connor were getting the bar ready for the evening's customers.

'We found a phone box for Rob,' said Sean, stirring a cup of tea, 'but it's a fair way from the road where he's on watch. He'd almost be quicker coming back home if he spots the van. Have a cuppa.'

Gilly said 'no thanks' and decided to go to the old factory and collect Marcia and Melanie. She knew that work on the building for that day would soon end and that Mr Galloway would lock up for the night.

On her way down Manton Street, she exchanged waves with Harry. As she came into the carpark, she noticed a large skip container had been placed in the far corner to hold the rubbish which the conversion of the building had produced.

Outside and inside, the new headquarters was looking very smart, now that work on it was nearly completed. The club office, canteen and changing rooms had been finished and the training pit was nearly ready. The newest piece of construction was the balcony for spectators, and Marcia and Melanie were helping to polish its guard rail. More new equipment – another vaulting horse, a pile of floor mats and a beam – had arrived.

If those crooks want to burn this lovely place down, they're completely crazy, thought Gilly as she approached Mr Galloway and a group of parents and helpers who were tidying up.

'Not long to go now, Gilly,' said Mr Galloway. 'We'll move the rest of the equipment in here next week.'

'It's looking great,' said Gilly. 'I can't wait to train here.'

She stood looking at the freshly-painted woodwork and the red curtains which she had helped to make. She glanced up to her friends on the balcony and noticed that a climbing rope from one of the roof girders had been attached to the guard rail to keep it out of the way. I wouldn't mind swinging down on that rope some time, she said to herself.

'Let's call it a day,' said Mr Galloway to all his workforce. 'I'll be here at ten if anyone wants to lend a hand tomorrow.'

Within a few minutes, the new headquarters were deserted. Mr Galloway, the last to leave apart from Gilly, Marcia and Melanie, locked the front door and drove away in his car.

'Any news?' asked Marcia as they walked along Manton Street to the Narrow Boat.

'None so far,' Gilly told her, 'but it's a little early, yet.'

It was beginning to get dark and Gilly wondered when the vandals would come, if they came at all. While the High Flyers and the Mobsters had been doing less patrolling in the area, the police and the club's watchdog committee still paid regular visits to Manton Street at night.

Gilly knew that it would be no problem for the two baddies to avoid any official patrol from the canal side of the old factory as long as they kept quiet. They could not, however, hear anyone waiting for them silently in the dark, as if in an ambush.

That could be us, thought Gilly. If they come.

At the Narrow Boat, there was no news either. Sean had sent Lofty and Pete to relieve Titch and Rob who arrived shortly afterwards. Shani had appeared again, but said she couldn't stay long.

The seven of them sat in the pub's kitchen, watching television but listening out for the sound of the telephone. They could hear the usual chatter and laughter from the bar, and once Mrs O'Connor put her head around the kitchen door.

'You lot all right?' she asked.

'We're fine, thank you,' said Gilly, wishing something would happen. She could sense her friends becoming impatient with waiting.

'This is boring,' declared Marcia. 'I'm going home soon.'

Before long, Gilly realized that if there was no

sign of the vandals by nine o'clock, they would have to go home before their parents started to worry. She was beginning to feel very tired after her adventures that day . . .

'Wake up, Gilly,' said Melanie. 'The phone's ringing.'

And so it was. Sean had leaped up and run into the passage by the bar to answer it. He was back within a minute.

'The van's left the yard,' he said excitedly. 'And Lofty's on his way.'

Everyone began to talk at once. All they needed now was a call from Pete in a few minutes time and they would know that the crooks were definitely heading for the club headquarters again. Then they could send for the police.

Gilly shivered from a mixture of excitement and fear. But several minutes passed and the phone still remained silent. As the time lengthened, so the feeling of impatience returned to the group. The talking dwindled to a stop.

At the end of half an hour, Sean glanced at the kitchen clock. 'Looks as if those men aren't coming after all. Old Pete should have rung by now.'

'Yeah,' said Rob, stretching and yawning. 'Let's pack it up.'

The back door opened and a breathless Lofty came in. He could tell at a glance that nothing had been heard from Pete.

'We're going home,' announced Melanie. There were murmurs of agreement.

140

Then Gilly had a sudden thought. 'Look. Lofty, was the van definitely carrying the canoe?'

'Yep, it was. Why?'

'Well, that must mean that the crooks *are* coming over here. I bet Pete somehow hasn't been able to phone through. And if that's so – '

'Jumping Jupiter,' interrupted Marcia, 'those men could be here already!'

'You're right,' said Sean grimly, 'let's get over there.'

'Wait,' said Gilly, 'if they are at the factory, we've got to get the police here – fast.'

Sean nodded. 'That's Lofty's job. Okay, my son? When I give the word, get on to Harry speediest. But stay out of sight.'

Lofty's eyes gleamed.

Gilly went on: 'Another thing, we can't all go down to the factory. We'll sound like a herd of elephants. Melanie, Shani and Rob – you better stay here for the moment. But come along fast if you hear any rumpus.'

'Good thinking,' said Sean. 'Right, troops. Let's go.'

Gilly, Marcia, Sean, Titch and Lofty slipped out of the Narrow Boat and crossed the street to the watchman's cabin.

Harry opened his window and peered at them. 'What are you little people up to? Club's closed long ago.'

Sean went up to him. 'Nothing to worry about, Harry,' he said in a low voice, 'we're just going to check the club building.'

141

Silently and cautiously, the group hurried down Manton Street. The dark had closed in fully and the further they moved away from the light of Harry's cabin, the more Gilly found the deserted neighbourhood spooky and sinister. A slight breeze made her feel colder than she was.

Sean peeped around the corner of the old factory. Then he waved the group on. They tiptoed across the carpark and settled down behind the skip, straining with their ears to catch any sound from the canal.

'How long – ' began Titch in a loud whisper.

'Shut up,' said Sean sharply. 'Just keep listening.'

Gilly began to feel shivers of fright again and her breathing became heavier. She hoped no one could hear her. Pull yourself together, she ordered herself, even if it's the scariest time of the last few weeks. If she had known what was going to happen to her when she joined the gym club . . .

Then the five heard a noise – a noise just over the canal wall which made them all fully alert.

There was a hollow bump, followed by a clatter of wood. The canoe's arrived – and someone's dropped a paddle, realized Gilly. Here we go . . .

She was right. A man's voice cursed in low tones and there was a scrambling sound as he climbed out of the canoe.

Another voice also cursed. 'For Heaven's sake, Fudger, pipe down! The whole flaming town will hear you!'

There was an answering grunt, then some more scrambling. Gilly and her friends, still crouched

142

rigidly behind the skip, guessed correctly that the man called Fudger was looking over the wall.

A voice that Gilly and Marcia had heard that very afternoon sounded hoarsely: 'Coast clear, matey. Let's have the crowbar.'

Sean stole a glance over the skip and saw that Fudger had climbed down again to the canoe. He gave Lofty a double pat on his arm, and the small boy's shape vanished speedily away into the darkness.

Fudger returned to climb the wall, once more noisily. He dropped into the carpark, clunking his long iron bar. He went up to the building and in a few moments levered the padlocks off the door and opened it with a splintering of wood. He then went back to the wall.

'Let's have the petrol, Mick,' he called, scrambling over the wall again. 'Door's open!'

Gilly straightened up. They *were* going to burn the building down. Something had to be done – immediately.

'Look,' she whispered to her friends, 'let's get inside and hide. Boys, go behind the equipment at the end of the gym. Marcia, get by the light switches inside the office door. When you hear me call, turn them all on. Then we've got to try and stop them before they set everything alight. Quick!'

With Fudger out of sight, the four crept out from behind the skip, crossed the carpark and entered the building. Although it was pitch black, everyone managed to find a hiding place without making too much noise. Sean and Titch crouched down behind

143

a pile of floor mats and a vaulting box. Gilly went upstairs to the balcony and sat down behind the guard rail. Then once more they waited, hearts pounding.

In a few moments, they heard heavy tramping of feet. The two men came into the gym, the leading one flashing a torch.

'Mick, for gawd's sake keep that light low,' growled the other man. 'We're not appearing in a pantomime. Now where's something we can set a match to.'

'One of them mats,' suggested his mate, shining his torch around the gym. 'A little dose of petrol – and we're away.' He picked up a mat from the top of the pile behind which Sean was hiding. Gilly closed her eyes and prayed.

Luck was with Sean. The man called Mick was so intent on picking up the floor mat that he failed to notice the boy crouching low like a tortoise in its shell. Gilly began to breathe again.

'Top of the class, friend,' said Fudger carrying the tin of petrol towards the balcony. 'Put it by this wall. Should go up really well.'

Gilly opened her mouth to scream.

Then the door to the gym slammed three times, the sound filling the wide space like three claps of thunder. The toughs froze in alarm.

'Flipping 'ell, what's that?' barked Fudger.

Gilly pulled air into her lungs. 'Now!' she yelled for as long as she could, sounding, as Marcia said afterwards, like a cat in pain.

144

The gym lights blazed on as Marcia flicked the switches and the men stood dazed in surprise.

For the first time, Gilly could see the vandals who had caused so much trouble to the Lincston Gymnastics Club. Both were about John's age and large in shape. The man called Mick wore dirty jeans and an old sweater but Fudger was crammed into the second yellow tracksuit which they had stolen from the club. Both were unshaven and had rough-looking, leering faces.

The boys came out from behind the equipment, waiting for the next move. The men spun around to face them and then turned quickly again as someone strode in from the front door. It was Pete. He stood defiantly just inside the gym, arms crossed. Good old Pete, thought Gilly. He must have realized what was going on and slammed the door – just at the right moment.

Marcia came out of the office and stood beside him, trying not to shake with fright. Then, to Gilly's surprise and delight, they were joined by the rest of their friends – Melanie, Shani, Hazel, Stephanie, Lofty and Rob.

'Bleeding kids!' snarled Mick, glaring at the waiting High Flyers and Manton Mobsters.

'Well, they ain't going to stop us,' said Fudger angrily. He poured petrol over the floor mat. 'We're still going to have a nice little bonfire!'

Chapter 13

The man called Mick pulled a cigarette lighter from his pocket and flicked it alight. Everyone in the gym stopped dead, looking at the tiny flame.

Then, without warning, Gilly swung down from the balcony at the end of the climbing rope which had been tethered there. With legs stretched in front of her, she careened into Mick and knocked him over like a tenpin. He went sprawling and lay bewildered on the floor of the gym. Gilly let go of the rope and dropped lightly down beside him, rolling over like a parachutist does on landing. She ran over to Sean and stood panting. Sean gave her a grin and took a step towards Fudger. The others did the same.

Fudger growled with rage and snatched up the crowbar, edging over to the fallen Mick.

We haven't a chance, thought Gilly desperately. 'Be careful, Sean!' she called.

'Frig off – or you'll get bashed!' threatened Fudger. He picked up his mate's cigarette lighter. 'Get up, son,' he called, 'we're going to show these brats what a real brew-up is!'

Mick groaned and got to his knees, watched by eleven worried faces.

Gilly's ears were on the alert for the sound that would mean help. Hurry, hurry, hurry, she begged to herself.

Then she heard it, the most welcome din in the whole world, the sirens of speeding police cars. The wails grew louder and through the windows of the old building came the welcoming flashes of blue lamps. The High Flyers and the Mobsters began to relax and smile at each other.

The two men looked quickly around the gym as if to discover some way they could escape. On realizing they were trapped, they stood waiting with the evidence of their attempted outrage around them –

a tin of petrol, a soaked floor mat, an iron crowbar, a cigarette lighter and a stolen yellow tracksuit.

When six police officers burst into the gym, Gilly burst into tears with relief.

Later, in the crowded kitchen of the Narrow Boat, Gilly explained to Inspector Graham and John Hanley just how they had discovered the whereabouts of the two vandals.

She produced the second tracksuit top which had been stolen from the new headquarters and Pete described how he had found it further down the canal. Shani then told her story of how she traced the van to the builder's yard.

Gilly wanted to know why Pete hadn't telephoned when the van approached the canal. She learned that after the van had passed him, a woman beat him to the telephone box. She just wouldn't stop talking and, with the time slipping by fast, Pete eventually decided to rush back to Manton Street in person. When he found his friends were inside with the crooks, he slammed the door three times . . .

Sean took over to relate just what happened when the two vandals arrived at the club's building.

'I had the heebie-jeebies,' said Marcia. 'But you should have seen Gilly swinging down on that rope . . .'

The others agreed. 'It was a-mazing,' said Rob. 'Yeah, just like a huge great monkey.'

There were howls of laughter and everyone began to feel cheerful again.

'You should have told us earlier about your discoveries,' said Inspector Graham, trying to sound official. 'It could have saved a lot of time.'

'The police weren't exactly in favour of us boys,' Sean pointed out. 'And I don't think anyone would have believed us until we had found clear proof that showed exactly who was up to no good.'

'I think that's fair enough, Inspector,' said John.

'These lads deserve an apology without a doubt,' said Mrs O'Connor as she brought over a fresh pot of tea.

'They do indeed,' admitted Inspector Graham, 'and more. They deserve a lot of thanks. But the case isn't over yet.'

'What do you mean?' asked John.

'We've got to find out who ordered the two men to damage your building. But that shouldn't take long.'

Shani's soft voice spoke up. 'Excusing me, I can show you.' She produced a photograph from her coat. 'I took this the other day at the yard.'

The picture showed Mick and Fudger listening carefully to a man in a suit.

'I'm blowed,' said John, 'that's Culverhay.' He explained to the policeman how the businessman had always wanted to own the old factory.

'I'll take this along if I may,' said the Inspector. He turned to Shani. 'Well done, young lady. Indeed, well done all of you.'

Shani shook her head. 'Please, it is Gilly who is really special. She worked everything out.'

Gilly blushed as a chorus of voices agreed.

'I go along with that,' said John. 'Thanks to Gilly, the club's going to be a far happier place from now on.'

'Hear, hear,' chirped Melanie.

'Now first things first,' continued John. 'All of you get straight back home now or there will be a lot of worried parents around my neck. And I mean *now*.'

Gilly arrived home a lot later than her usual bedtime and was not surprised to find her parents waiting for her. She half expected them to be cross, but both of them seemed thankful to see her.

Gilly started to tell them about her experiences that evening but Mrs Denham interrupted her.

'That can wait until tomorrow, darling,' she said. 'John Hanley's just rung us. You get off to bed.'

'Sleep well, Gilly Denham,' said her father with pride in his voice. 'From now on, everything's going to go just right for you.'

But I still do have a big problem, thought Gilly as her mother tucked her up in bed. I've got to get into the elite squad and heaven knows that's not going to be easy . . .

'Good night, God bless,' said Mrs Denham, turning off the light. 'Have a lie-in tomorrow and then we can sort out anything that still needs to be sorted out.'

Sunday turned out to be a very busy day. Inspector Graham dropped in to ask more questions and make further notes. Christine passed by with a big box of chocolates and a photographer from the local newspaper took her picture. Then John and Mr Bennett, president of the gym club, came over and Gilly had to tell her story yet again. Someone delivered a bunch of flowers and the telephone

150

never seemed to stop ringing, with people calling to congratulate her.

'That was Mr Galloway,' said her father sounding pleased after a particularly long telephone call. 'He says "top of the pops" to you and that the club's central heating is working superbly.'

Finally, after lunch, Gilly made her escape and went over to the Cherrys' where she and Marcia listened to music tapes for the rest of the afternoon.

'You know,' said Marcia with a giggle, 'the parents of Lyn Hobday and Veronica Tatlow have asked whether their girls can join the club again. I bet they don't get a quick answer on that one.'

'I wonder what Caroline Mayhew is thinking,' said Gilly. 'I suppose she won't be exactly chuffed.'

At the Tuesday training session of the gym club, Caroline Mayhew looked very subdued indeed. She and her friends watched in embarrassed silence as the other members of the novice squad crowded delightedly around the High Flyers, wanting to hear their adventures first-hand. Several coaches had words of praise for the five girls, too.

John had to be firm to get the warm-up started. 'There's plenty of time for nattering afterwards,' he called. 'Remember, you've got an important competition on Saturday.'

Nothing had been closer to Gilly's mind than the novice competition, now that she was allowed to compete after her Award 1 success. Only seven novices would be permitted to join the elite squad at this time and Gilly knew only too well that her setback had lessened her chances of becoming an elite member.

After the warm-up, Christine went over the rules of the competition once more. As well as one vault, the handspring, each novice had to perform a simple one-minute floor exercise using movements she had learned in the awards scheme. The movements could be performed in any order as long as they were in harmony with a recorded piece of piano music which every girl by now knew by heart.

'If I hear that tune again, I swear I'll go crackers,' whispered Marcia to Gilly.

Christine told the girls that they could use the rest of the evening working out their routine and thankfully Gilly made some notes as she planned out what she was going to do. She knew that one of the secrets of a successful floor exercise was to link each move smoothly and naturally. She would start crouched down, and then spring up into two back flips . . . This time, she was in competition with Marcia and so she had to work out her routine by herself.

By Saturday morning, her floor sequence was etched in her brain. She knew it had to be flowing and not too rushed. At the church hall, she went off into a corner to concentrate hard by herself before she was called out to perform her routine.

John announced that everyone would perform in alphabetical order and that the results would be given out at the opening of the club's new head-quarters next week so that time could be given to the assessment of each novice.

152

He also said that the three best girls would perform their routines as part of the club's display that evening. The novices were already going to demonstrate some basic tumbling and vaulting skills.

The hall grew still as the competition started. First, each novice performed her handspring vault and then waited to tackle her floor exercise. Marcia and Stephanie were on before Gilly and both sailed through their routine easily, attracting the quiet approval of their fellow-gymnasts.

Marcia makes every movement look so simple, thought Gilly with a touch of envy.

'Gilly Denham,' called Christine.

Aware of all eyes watching her, Gilly crouched down on the large floor mat. For once, she felt relaxed and in command of herself.

The music started – and as she sprang up, Gilly knew for the first time what it really meant to be a gymnast. The exercise enveloped her in one big expression of happiness and achievement which was hers to show and hers alone.

The sequence carried her along in a wave of pleasure – two back flips, round-off, kick to handstand, handstand forward roll, handspring . . . She included turns, jumps and pirouettes, forward and sideways splits and used the entire area of the mat. Everyone watching could feel her enjoyment and there was a ripple of applause when she finished as she began – with two back flips and a round-off.

'Reckon you're definitely in the elite squad, Gilly Denham,' said Marcia afterwards. 'You were really

153

zingy, you were. It's a swizz we won't know who's in until next week, though.'

Gilly was still feeling the thrilling effect of her floor exercise. I don't really mind what happens now, she thought. I did my best and if I can do that again, that's all I want – in the elite squad or not.

But by the time of the official opening, her longing to join the elite squad was stronger than ever. She began to go over every move of her floor exercise in her mind, wondering whether she had made any serious mistakes.

'You're a bit po-faced, my girl,' said Mr Denham as he drove his family down to Manton Street. 'I hope you're going to enjoy this evening.'

'Yeah, cheer up, old toad,' said Richard. 'We're not going to a funeral.' He had been accepted for the new boys' section at the club and he could hardly wait to begin training.

'Thank you, gentlemen,' said Gilly primly. 'I'm perfectly all right.'

But her mood changed to one of excitement as they turned by the Narrow Boat into Manton Street. For once, the street was filled with parked cars. The old factory was ablaze with lights and outside the front door was a gleaming new sign with the familiar yellow head of a lynx and the words 'Lincston Gymnastics Club'.

Inside, the newly-decorated gym was packed with gymnasts, coaches, parents, friends and guests. The balcony was also full of spectators and beneath it, Mrs O'Connor and some mothers of gymnasts were

154

arranging tables loaded with food, drink and bunches of flowers.

'Hello, Denhams,' said a cheerful voice. It was Mr Galloway. 'I'll show you to your seats.' He led Mr and Mrs Denham and Richard away to a row under the windows.

Gilly slipped off to join Marcia on the benches at the end of the gym where the club members were crowded together. From there, she spotted the five Manton Mobsters, all far tidier than she had ever known them, sitting with old Harry, the night watchman. Sean had lost his scowl completely, she thought. Looking around, she noticed Inspector Graham in the audience as well.

Marcia tapped her. 'Look, Veronica Tatlow and Lynn Hobday are back with us. At least that's going to strengthen our senior team.'

Gilly was about to agree when everyone stood up. Mr Bennett led in a small party which included a stout man with a gold chain around his neck, his wife, and John Hanley.

'That's the mayor of Lincston,' whispered Marcia.

Mr Bennett and John led the mayor to the middle of the floor area, while the others took their seats near the Denhams.

'Please sit down,' said Mr Bennett. After everyone had made themselves comfortable, he went on: 'We're here to enjoy ourselves, not to listen to speeches. But before I ask his worship the mayor to declare our new headquarters open, I would like to say thanks on behalf of the club to some young people whose praiseworthy efforts foiled a serious

155

attempt to deprive us of this building. Without them, indeed, we would not be here tonight.'

'I therefore call on the following to come out here – Robert Wilson, Michael Evans, Peter Mactear, David Pratt and Sean O'Connor.'

'Who on earth are they?' asked Marcia.

'The Manton Mobsters, idiot,' said Gilly with a laugh.

Then their names were announced with those of Hazel, Shani, Melanie and Stephanie. With sheepish grins, they all lined up in front of the mayor who shook hands with them.

Briefly, Mr Bennett told the audience of the patrolling, investigating and action by the eleven youngsters which had undoubtedly saved the building if not the club. He also pointed out that at one time several of them had been under suspicion of being connected with the vandalism and the club would like to say 'sorry' as well as 'thanks'.

There was a huge outbreak of applause and cheers. When it had died down, John stepped forward. 'Now that the club has moved here,' he said, 'our new boys' section can be started. As many of you may know, we have asked these boys to be founder-members and I take great pleasure in welcoming them here.'

After a further round of applause, Gilly and her friends went back to their seats, glowing with happiness.

The mayor then made a short speech, wishing the club a happy future, and declared the new headquarters officially opened.

Everyone clapped for a long time as that moment marked the end of a long period of great efforts and many disappointments. Ahead, there lay more hard work, of course, but hard work which had the goal of making Lincston Gymnastics Club one of the most successful in the region, if not the country.

'Now we'll have the display,' said Gilly to Marcia. But she was mistaken.

John Hanley put up his hands for silence. 'Before we carry on,' he told the audience, 'there are two important things which I have to do. The first is to announce the seven girls in the novice squad who have earned promotion to the elite squad.'

He consulted a piece of paper. The gym grew still. 'They are, in order of excellence – Marcia Cherry, Gilly Denham, Toni Williamson, Caroline Mayhew, Vanessa Dugdale, Shani Patel and Deidre Nicholson.'

Marcia and Gilly gave shrieks of delight as once more the applause broke out around them.

'I don't believe it,' cried Marcia, 'the old firm of Cherry and Denham – one and two!'

No other news could have thrilled Gilly more as she never expected to do so well, but she was sad that Hazel, Melanie and Stephanie would have to wait before they, too, joined the elite squad. Deep down inside her, she knew that it would not take them long.

On the other side of the gym, Mrs Denham wiped a tear away from her eye.

John stood still, waiting for the noise to die down. When the gym was silent, he continued. 'I'd like

157

Marcia, Gilly and Toni to show you their respective floor exercises later. But before we march on for our display, I would like to tell you about my second duty. Every year, the club presents awards to its gymnasts who have done particularly well, and during the display which you are about to see, our best girls will receive trophies for their achievements.

'But there is one award which I am going to present now which we at Lynx regard as something very special. It does not necessarily go to a gymnast for high standards of performance, but rather to the club member who has unselfishly done the most for the entire club during the year. This year, one gymnast stands out from everyone, a gymnast whom we all can regard with much gratitude and pride.'

John looked across to Christine who brought him a small silver cup. 'For total determination and pluck, I am delighted to present this well-deserved award to – Gilly Denham.'

Gilly was stunned with surprise and disbelief. She staggered to her feet and went towards John, seeing everything in a blur. The applause broke out around her and hammered into her ears. She was barely aware of John pressing the cup into her hands and her friends, no longer able to sit still, rushing out on to the mat to surround and lift her.

The march boomed out through the loudspeakers and for the first time the girls of Lincston Gymnastics Club, their heads held high, swung into the gymnasium of the club's new headquarters. The spectators clapped their hands in time to the music as

158

the long line of yellow leotards entered proudly into the hallway.

Gilly Denham marched in front of Marcia Cherry. Her mind was flashing the same message again and again: Walk tall, Gymnast Gilly – you've arrived here at last.